Eva Bell Botsford

Lucky

A Tale of the Western Prairie

Eva Bell Botsford

Lucky
A Tale of the Western Prairie

ISBN/EAN: 9783743393714

Manufactured in Europe, USA, Canada, Australia, Japa

Cover: Foto ©Andreas Hilbeck / pixelio.de

Manufactured and distributed by brebook publishing software (www.brebook.com)

Eva Bell Botsford

Lucky

LUCKY

A Tale of the Western Prairie

BY

EVA BELL BOTSFORD

" Words are tiny drops of Ink."—Anon.

BUFFALO
THE PETER PAUL BOOK COMPANY
1895

CONTENTS

LUCKY—A TALE OF THE WESTERN PRAIRIE.

CHAPTER I.

A LILY AMONG WEEDS.

THE great, pompous, red-faced sun came up from
behind the little green hills, and the cackle of
ducks from the region of the rush-grown ravine
greeted his advent. The farm hands were bringing
out their breaking ploughs from the machine shed,
whistling stray snatches of dance music and love
songs. Two buxom girls in pink calico sun-bonnets
stood beside some pails of foaming milk, guarding it
from the ravages of pigs and chickens until the arrival
of the man whose mission was to convey it to the vats
in the dairy house. The cattle were leisurely making
their way through the wide open gate of the spacious
pine-board corral, quite indifferent to the "Whoop
halloo! G'lang there!" of the herd boy, which rang
out sonorously upon the air, accompanied by the
cracking of an immense whip wielded with more
ostentation than purpose. They knew the whip and
its owner, and were not afraid of its sting.

Ninety sleek milch cows were there in the herd, of
various sizes and colors. There was a mild-eyed dun
beauty with white spots on her flanks, a noble roan
with a line along her back, and a coquettish little
speckled heifer with spiked horns; but the queen of the
herd was a superb black creature with a star on her

brow who carried her head with a proud air as if con-
scious of superior distinction. Slowly they lagged,
nipping at the tender grass as they went, while the herd
boy rode to and fro on his ginger-colored pony, vainly
shouting and flourishing his formidable whip.

This was the dairy farm of the Roysters. To the
right of the corral was the spring, noted far and wide
for its water of icy coldness, walled up with limestone
and shaded by overhanging willows. It was the pride
of the farm. To the south, were the barns and sheds,
while to the west stood the dairy house, or cheese
house, as it was more commonly called, an immense
frame structure painted pale yellow like the cheeses it
contained; to the right of that, was a quaint L shaped
building known as the "House." In this latter place
Mrs. Royster held her august sway and also the
official position of postmistress for the settlement, that
honor having been thrust upon her because no one
else would have it.

By the spring stood a child of some ten or. eleven
years of age, dressed in a loose gown of coarse, brown
ducking. Her feet were bare and scarred by daily
contact with stone and stubble. This was Nana
Meers, adopted daughter, bound child, ward, or nobody knew what, of the Roysters. She was beautiful,
not with the soft outlines and fresh tints of the ordi-
narily pretty child, but wildly, defiantly dark and
lovely. Her arms were full of long trailing rush
blades, and a sober smile stole into her great eyes, as
she stroked the green, glossy, ribbon-like things, with

one little brown palm. The look changed when the herd boy rode past. It became intense and eager. She flew to him, and put her hand entreatingly upon his stirrup.

"What is it, young 'un?" came the gruff query.

"Oh Lund, you won't forget to get my almanick, now will you?" she coaxed plaintively.

"Not if I think of it," was the curt reply, and the boy drove his cattle away, over the hills and out of sight.

The child, however, was contented. She returned to the shade of the willows and sat down musing. "I'm going to have a almanick! Won't it be awful splendid! It won't be a old one, but bran' new with white, shiny leaves, and it won't be a borrered one, but all mine, mine, mine! If Lund don't forget it, it will, and I guess he won't."

Presently, a head appeared at one of the upper windows of the house. Nana started when she saw it, dropping some of the rush blades into the spring.

"See here! You get away from that spring with your rubbish, you imp!" was the greeting of the new-comer.

"I ain't a imp!" came the prompt reply, "and I'm glad I spilled 'em in the spring!"

"Take care how you talk to me."

"But I ain't!"

"Didn't I say shut up?"

"But I ain't!"

"I'll come down there and larrup you if you say that again!"

"If you do, I'll kill you!"

"Haw! Haw! Haw! Talk about killin', you little slim snipe!"

"But I will—I'll choke you to death!"

"Haw! Haw! Haw!"

"Stop laughin' at me, you big—big brute!"

"Look a' here, young one, you're a gettin' a little too sassy. Dry up, and go tend your ducks."

"I won't tend the ducks, and I'll put more stuff in the spring if I want to."

The child with a determined toss of the head arose, and started to run away. She had not proceeded far, however, when she heard heavy footfalls behind her, and soon a rough hand grasped her shoulder.

"Say that again!" hissed a voice in her ear.

"I will if I want to."

The hand tightened its grasp. Nana turned, and struck at her tormentor with her little brown fist, at which he laughed exasperatingly. If strength of spirit could slay, Bub Royster in one second would have been no more. As it was, Nana could only battle in the cause of justice with feet, teeth, and nails, which she did right manfully. Bub Royster only laughed the more.

"Now, see here. I'm going to drown you for your impudence," he said at last, when tired of the sport. Nana struggled while he dragged her to the edge of the spring; but soon her fragile form relaxed, and she felt her head thrust beneath the surface. Then she fainted from exhaustion and fright.

When she recovered consciousness, she was lying on the grass, her dress wet from the water which dripped from her curls, and a woman in high, metallic voice was saying:

"What do you mean by duckin' her in there, and sp'ilin' the water?"

"She called me names," said Bub.

"Well, you jist stop this onery behavin' or I'll tell your pap."

Nana sat up, and laughed aloud. Oh, it is a rare day when we see those who have made us suffer discomfited in turn!

The woman hearing the uncontrollable merriment, turned upon the child.

"Here you ugly sprite, you get out of here, and go to your ducks, or I'll make you laugh out of the other corner of your mouth. You ought to be in the Deform School, and you'll get sent there too, first thing you know!"

Not caring to match her strength with any one else this morning, Nana scampered away, but once out of sight and hearing, she paused, and her little face turned livid with rage and indignation.

"If I could only kill them Roysters!" she exclaimed, stamping her foot. Then a sudden thought struck her. Falling upon her knees, she clasped her hands and prayed.

"O God, I hate 'em all, Bub and Mis' Royster and all, and I want you to come and kill 'em, dead, dead, dead— all but Lund— he's going to get me a almanick. Amen."

"I guess they're fixed now," she said as she arose.

The ducks were an exceedingly wild species and required constant watching, lest they should wander away and join the nomadic flocks which daily flew over the farm, now and then pausing to visit their more domestic brothers and sisters, and express their contempt for civilization. The Roysters, however, need not care, since they were to suffer annihilation so soon. The sun was warm and the atmosphere lazy. Nana threw herself down among the tall grasses, and let the ducks go their way. When time came for returning home, she could find but half the flock.

She forebore to search for them. The Roysters might beat her to-day for her carelessness, but they never would again. They were going to die.

As she had expected, soon after her return, Mrs. Royster's stout cottonwood switch was called into requisition. Nana did not cry when the blows rained down upon her tender shoulders. She was triumphing in her sincere belief that the sway of the tyrant was brief. Mrs. Royster was nonplussed.

"Oh, it don't hurt, don't it? Well, I'll give you something that will!" and the blows fell thicker and faster. Then Nana wept for the sake of policy, all the while her heart was exulting.

"Oh, Lund!" she cried to the herd boy, as he came toiling tired and hungry up the path. "I want to tell you something. It's a nawful secret!"

"Well, what is it!"

"By to-morrer morning, the Roysters will all be

dead!'' she answered in a whisper not untinged with awe.

"The young 'un's crazy," Lund muttered.

"No I aint, and you'll see for yourself— and oh, Lund, did you get my almanick?"

"No. Forgot it. Come on to supper."

But Nana did not care for supper. That almanac had been the desire of her heart for days. The Royster family had no books, not even a bible, and the almanac, especially if there were pictures, contained for the lonely child, food for a whole year of dreams. She crept up to her ragged bed in the garret under the rafters, to sob out her disappointment. She had not been there long when a rough, though not unkindly voice called:

"Nane!"

The girl sat up and dried her tears.

"It's Lund! Maybe he has been teasing me, and has brought the almanick, after all! Oh, Lund, where is it?" holding out her hand.

"Here," said Lund, depositing in the outstretched palm, a huge piece of corn-bread savored with sorghum molasses.

"Oh, no, not that!"

"Well, what did you expect? Apple-pie and plum-puddin?"

"No, no! I only want my almanick!" she sobbed.

"I—I forgot it," stammered Lund. I didn't go near the burg to-day. I didn't know you cared so much. What do you want an almanick for anyway, kid?"

"Oh, Lund, they are de-light-ful! Such pictures, and such readin'.''

"Well, I'll go to-morrer, cross my heart, I will!"

"Bless you, Lund!" and Nana threw her arms about the boy's neck, and kissed him.

"Oh my! The girl is crazy shore enough!" muttered Lund. "But," he observed, after a little reflection, "I don't know but I like such craziness, after all."

"You, Lundy!" called Mrs. Royster sharply, from below.

"I must go; Mis' Royster's a callin'," said Lund reluctantly.

"What are you a doin' a wastin' ot you time up there? Come down here this minute, or I'll pack you right off to the Perform School! There's the young calves to feed, and the turkeys to shut up, and the kindlin' to get in 'gainst mornin'. What with you and that shiftless girl a shirkin' of your work, I'll be driv' to my grave," the voice continued.

"Good-bye, kid. Sorry I can't stay," said Lund.

"You won't forget to remember to-morrer," the girl asked, creeping close to him, and laying her cheek against his ragged sleeve.

"Catch me a forgettin'."

"If you aint the laziest, good for nothingest rascal that ever lived! I—" from below.

"Yes'm, yes'm," answered Lund promptly, thus pouring oil on the troubled waters.

An hour later every one on the farm was asleep

except the boy. He was tossing to and fro on his hard bed saying over and over to himself:

"She did take it hard didn't she? Well, I'll get it for her to-morrer, shore. Pore little kid!"

CHAPTER II.

A DREAMING GIRL AND A PRAIRIE KNIGHT.

"YOU, Lundy!"

"W-h-a-a-t?" was the drowsy reply.

"Is that the way to speak to me, you pack o' lazy bones? Why don't you say, 'what mum' to your betters!"

"What mum?" repeated Lund obediently.

"You jest stir your stumps now and mount up to that loft, and tell that girl to be up and about a searchin' for them ducks, for I swear she shan't have a bite to eat till I see them, every blessed one before my very eyes."

Having issued these peremptory orders, Mrs. Royster went her way singing:

"How tedious and tasteless the hour."

She did not know the hymn and never got beyond the first line, following out the air with a cracked and doleful hum. The farm hands averred that she made many an hour tedious and tasteless for them with that hum.

Lund opened his eyes, surprised to find it morning so soon. He arose and dressed, then climbed the shaky ladder very softly, lest he should awaken the sleeper a moment before he must. Lund's hours of

slumber were dear to him, being as they were the hap-
piest of his life, and it seemed cruel to rouse the girl
from sweet unconsciousness to ugly hard reality.   Besides, Nana had become an especial object of consider-
ation to him since the previous night.   No one but
she had ever kissed him since the day his mother had
been laid to rest in the back woods of Iowa.

"Nane!" he called gently, perking his head up
over the floor of the loft.   No answer.

"Nane!" still louder.

"H-e-y?" from the corner where Nana lay, half
asleep, half awake.

"Mis' Royster says—"

"Aint she dead yet?" inquired the drowsy Nana.

"Dead, Nane?   What do you mean?"

"Just what I say.   Well, if she ain't, she will be
soon.   Tell her I'm comin'."

Not long after, Nana came into the little bare apartment which served as dining-room and kitchen in one,
where the farm hands were devouring their morning
repast.

"You get out o' here," was Mrs. Royster's greeting.

"I won't till I've had my breakfast," declared Nana.

"You won't!   Well, we'll see," Mrs. Royster
returned, accompanying her remark with a sound box
on Nana's ear.

The farm hands laughed.   Mrs. Royster gave them
an approving look.

"See there.   They're laughin' at you, spunky, and
well you deserve it.   Now get."

"I don't care how much they laugh. They're just as bad as you are, and I hate 'em just as much, and I'm going to have something to eat," said Nana, seizing a plate of corn bread that stood within reach.

"Oh, you will, will you?" exclaimed Mrs. Royster, "We'll see about that."

She caught Nana's hand, and tried to wrest the bread from her, but the child clung to it as an animal clings to its prey.

"I'll fix you!" exclaimed Mr. Royster, coming in just in time to witness the disturbance. "You are gettin' a bit too sassy to the folks that feed and clothe you and teach you manners." With this, he snatched the food from her hand, and, thrusting her out, closed the door upon her.

The next moment an unearthly scream rent the air, and looking in the direction whence it came, they saw Nana, peering through the window, shaking her fist with intense violence, her face livid, her eyes aflame, and her slight figure quivering from head to foot.

"Ah," she cried, through her clenched teeth, "You'd better be down on your knees a sayin' your prayers from now on, for you aint long for this world, none of you!"

"What ails the young one?" said Mrs. Royster, as Nana vanished.

"She's mad," said Mr. Royster. "She needs that taken out of her, and by the old Harry, she'll get it done too."

"She's an awful young one," said the girl who waited on the farm hands.

"Terrible !" echoed the hands.

"She's half crazy," said Bub Royster.

"She ought to have been sent to the Inform School long afore this," said his mother.

Lund, who was at the table, listened silently ; but his food stuck in his throat, and refused to be washed down by constant deluges of water from his tin cup.

"What's the matter, boy? Your face is as red as a beet," remarked the man who sat next to him.

"Nothin'," muttered Lund dropping his eyes.

"Tryin' to eat too fast. Don't be afraid; you'll get enough, greedy," said Mrs. Royster.

When he went out, Lund found Nana sitting in a disconsolate attitude in her accustomed place under the willows by the spring. He had his dinner-bag in his hand. He threw it into her lap.

"There, Nane," he said, "take it and run for your life. They'll half kill you if they find you here."

"But you won't have any, then."

"I don't care. I'm a boy. I don't get hungry."

The tears rose to Nana's eyes.

"I won't take it at all, Lund, dear. Here's half of it back. Now, I'll scoot, and before I get back they'll all be dead. Won't we have good old times when they're gone? Don't forget the almanick."

*   *   *   *   *   *

The long grass swayed to and fro with a sleepy sound; the lithe dragon-fly hovered over the little pools of stagnant water, beside which the child lay with half-closed eyes, watching the graceful darting hither and thither of the pretty creatures on their transparent wings.

"I wonder why they stay around those ugly puddles," she mused dreamily. "If I had wings, I'd fly away to where everything was nice." Then, as the low, mournful call of the prairie gopher fell upon her ear, she reflected : "What makes him feel so bad ? He must have lost friends that he can't forget. I never had any friends, so I feel bad like him. Poor thing !"

At intervals a freight-line teamster passed down the great road, which, in the parlance of the West, led from "Omaha to Idaho." Nana could hear the creak of the oxen's yoke and the snap of the driver's whip. The teamsters were called bull-whackers, and Nana never quite overcame her dread of them. Every time she heard their rasping "Whoa, haw," she crouched farther down in the grass to hide. She believed them terrible creatures, in whom the spirit of torture was instinctive, and whose chief delight was to mistreat the poor dumb animals which they drove. It had been the custom of Mrs. Royster when the child was younger to frighten her into submission by the threat, "I'll give you to the bull-whackers." Now, despite her endeavor to keep well out of sight, one of them had espied her.

"Hello there, little 'un!" he cried, stopping his wagon, "What do you know? I am dogoned thirsty, and want a drink. There's water there I should say, by the rushes."

Nana's heart beat wildly, but she was determined

not to show her fear. She pointed out to him a little spring that she had hollowed out of a bank with her own hands, aided by a piece of broken milk crock.

"Gee, that's good!" exclaimed the man, when he had quenched his thirst. "Little 'un, you are a trump. What's better than a drink o' cold water to a man that's dry? Good-bye, chick. If you ever come to the city where I live you must make me a visit, shore. I've two or several little girls like you, and I think a heap of 'em. Here's a paper of goodies one of 'em stuck in my pocket th' other day, when I left. I aint much of a sweet tooth myself, and I'll give 'em to you."

Nana took the package with a half audible "thank'e, sir," as she had been taught. The man went on, and the little girl sat down to examine the gift. It proved to be ginger snaps. Better than all, the paper in which they were wrapped contained a wonderful story, which suited her appetite also. It was about a noble man who expended his immense wealth in founding colleges and building schools for orphan children such as she. Dr. Eustace was the gentleman's name. He cured the sick too, with a wonderful remedy known as Dr. Eustace's Miraculous Compound. Many a young man, the story said, had received a start in business from this benevolent gentleman, whose chief thought in life was to do good to his fellow creatures.

"I wonder if he would do anything for me," meditated Nana. "What a good man he must be!"

Her dreams were cut short by the sound of a voice, singing lustily :

"Old Missouri, souri, soo,
Old Missouri ay,
Old Missouri is the place
For you and I."

There was a rustle among the rushes and a step near at hand.

"Wall, I never !" broke from the lips of the new-comer.

"Nana looked up sullenly. He was a neighbor, a bachelor, who lived all alone on his claim, some miles distant. He had a broad jaw covered by a thin, stubby beard, a hair lip, small fish-like eyes, hulking body, and ambling gait. Nana despised him, and took pains to show it.

"Wall, I never !" he repeated. " I go out to find wild game, and run right onto a tame gal. Or ben't you tame, little 'un ? I swow I can't tell by the looks of you."

Nana did not condescend to reply. Joe Slocum, for that was the man's name, placed the butt end of his gun upon the ground, and leaned against the barrel, regarding the child with much amusement.

"Wall, my gal!" he said at length in the same jocular tone, " when air you goin' to marry me ? "

Nana immediately found voice.

" Marry you! I aint goin' to at all! "

" Yes, you air."

" No, I aint."

The man laughed exasperatingly.

"Your pap give you to me."

Her ire was now thoroughly roused.

"Go away!" she cried, stamping her feet. "I aint got any pap, and you are tellin' lies."

"No I aint, and you'll be glad on't too, when you come to keep house for me in my little shanty. I'm a good marksman, and you'll have plenty of prairie birds to cook. It'll be mighty fine."

"But I aint, I aint," protested Nana.

"Yes you air—oh, no you aint, kid, if you're goin' to look so glum about it—not till the time comes anyway. What air you a doin' of here?"

"None of your business. I've lost my ducks, and they have sent me out to hunt 'em up."

"Let 'em alone and they'll come home, a waggin' their tails behind 'em," chuckled Slocum.

"Shall I find your birds for you?" he inquired presently. "I'll warrant I can."

He was off without delay, but returned shortly with a string of game over his arm, which he flung at her feet.

"There you air. They went out in the mornin', I'll warrant, as noisy and gossipy as a lot o' gals, but they come back as quiet a pack o' fowl as I ever see."

Nana looked at them ruefully.

"I'll make it all right with the old man and old woman," suggested Slocum.

Still Nana did not speak. She kept gazing at the mute, inglorious birds.

"What time will you go home?" questioned the man.

"At dinner time," and her hungry eyes wandered towards the sun.

"I'll be there," said Slocum, and walked away.

*   *   *   *   *   *

"What, Nana Meers! The ducks are dead! What can you mean?" exclaimed Mrs. Royster when Nana had imparted the news to her.

"They are dead, that's all," said Nana doggedly. "Give me my dinner."

"You shall never have another bite, you—"

"Yes, she shall too," interposed a voice, the voice of Joe Slocum. He had come up unperceived by both Mrs. Royster and the girl.

"Here, I'll pay for the birds. I shot 'em. Give the gal her dinner. Air you goin' to?"

"Yes, but I'll lick her first!" cried the woman, making a spring at Nana.

"Not if I know it," answered the man, placing himself in front of the child.

Mrs. Royster looked thunder clouds at the intruder.

"I'd like to know what business it is of yours, Joe Slocum," she ejaculated fiercely. "Don't I house and keep her?"

"Yes," said Slocum impressively drawing close to his angry neighbor, "but I'll tell you what; the gal's mine. You give her to me, and she's mine, and I aint goin' to have her sp'iled by thrashin' nor starvin' neither. You jest put that in your pipe."

Mrs. Royster was somewhat appeased, but muttered something about encouraging the young imp in her bad ways.

"See here, chick," said Slocum, turning to Nana, "if this here woman don't treat you well, you jest come to me. Now, will you?"

Nana did something quite unexpected by both enemy and friend. She turned upon the good Samaritan with,

"No, I won't! Not if she beats me into the ground, I won't—not if she starves me dead!"

CHAPTER III.

FOLK LORE AND THE NEW NEIGHBORS.

"YES, I know, or I think I do."

The speaker was Lund. Nana had just told him of her interview with Joe Slocum.

"Well?" said the girl impatiently, as the boy paused a moment studying the proceedings of a swarm of ants that were bustling about a hill at his feet.

"Well," continued Lund thoughtfully, "it was the day I was sick and couldn't herd. Joe Slocum came over to see about ridin' to town with Royster next time he went with a load of cheese, and I heard them talkin'. I was hidin' under the big vat in the cheese house for fear some one would find me and set me to work, and I heard Royster tell old Slocum that as soon as you were big enough, Slocum could pay Royster three-hundred-dollars for your keep, and marry you. Then they shook hands, and took a drink out of the bottle that Royster keeps under a big canister in the cheese house."

"Did they say any more?"

"No. Just then I had to sneeze, and Slocum come and pulled me out from under the vat. But Royster said 'don't be afeard of the boy. He won't blab.' And he winked and put his front finger on his forehead."

"Well," said Nana firmly, "I think I see myself marryin' Joe Slocum."

"Won't you have to?"

Nana threw up her chin, and answered by repeating the old, iron-clad adage of the bullwhackers, "We don't have to do anything but die."

"Oh, Nane! Such a girl! I wonder if you really be crazy. Half the people say you be."

"Pooh! They're crazy themselves. It's all because I take my own part. Now you, Lund, you are good; you never sass or talk back, and you're never called crazy. But between you and me," she went on assuringly, "you are the craziest of the two."

Lund was half convinced.

"But it's an awful thing to die," he hesitated at length.

"Yes, for bad folks. For good ones it's nice."

"But you ain't good. Everybody says you ain't."

"Maybe I ain't. I don't care if I ain't. The Lord knows what I have to put up with. He'll excuse me."

"Maybe he will," said Lund with a sigh of relief, "I hope he will."

"What's this, my sharpies?" called a cheery voice hard by. Both children started at the sound.

"I've been laying for prairie chickens, but your gabble scares them all away," the stranger went on. "So you're discussing theology, are you?"

"No, we're talkin' about dyin'," said Lund.

"Your conversation savored of the science which I

name. Now, you leave all these vexing questions to
me, for I have a diploma at home, three feet square,
which proves that I'm fully capable of deciding.''
He was proud of his superior knowledge and experience, this handsome, dashing fellow, who stood nearly
six feet in his short jacket, high boots, and corduroy
trousers. You could see it in his entire bearing, but
more especially in the arrogant, backward tilt of his
broad sombrero, which disclosed to view an open,
genial brow over which the short, brown curls tumbled
in a very becoming confusion. He had a merry hazel
eye and large, mobile lips forever threatening to smile,
but seldom getting beyond the threat. He carried a
gun, game bag, and powder horn.

His name was George Fielding, but he was commonly
called ''Lucky,'' for it was his favorite boast that life
for him was one jolly round of gayety. He never
undertook anything which he failed to accomplish, was
accustomed to the admiration which success and good
looks are sure to bring and was somewhat spoiled by
always having had his own way. He possessed one
glaring fault, a strange, unconquerable disposition to
pervert the truth, to lie with so sober a front that even
the most penetrating reader of character would have
sworn he spoke gospel facts. His friends attributed it
to a vivid imagination, and he was so good natured
withal, that his grave failing was in the main, overlooked.

''Theology,'' he went on to explain to the two
wondering innocents, ''that means the science of

religion. The real thing and the science must not be confounded. I know plenty of people who have theology by the headful, without a speck of religion in their hearts. I knew a woman once who could talk doctrine by the hour, tell you to a T how many rods you'd strayed from the path of righteousness, had measured the gate of heaven with a tape line, and knew how many steps exactly there were to the golden stair. Why, any one would have supposed by the way she talked that she had even tested the temperature of the river Jordan. She always hollered in meeting. Young folks of the worldly sort used to go for miles to hear her holler. And what do you suppose she did, one day? She beat her horse to death for eating a turnip or two out of her cart. She had theology. Now I'll tell you another story of a woman who had religion. You couldn't have told she had anything by her looks or conversation. People thought her very bad because she never professed in public. But somehow, wherever a kind word or a helping hand was needed that woman was there, first of all to put her shoulder to the wheel. She gave all the cabbages and turnips she could spare to the poor, and I've no doubt, would have gone hungry herself rather than to see anyone suffer. She had a temper of her own too. Yet when she felt cross and wicked, she never laid the blame at the poor, much belied old devil's door, but took a good dose of herbs to tone up her system, smiled and went on as before. When she died, her neighbors shook their heads. She was

such a good soul, it was too bad she had never professed, they said.   Then they sighed and agreed to
leave her in the hands of the the Lord, to dispose of
according to His own mercy, since they could not help
themselves.''

"Of course the Lord knew," said Lund gravely.

"That he did, my hearty! He knew!"

The young man was beginning to glow with his
favorite theme.

"What brought sin into the world?" asked Nana.
"Royster always says it was women, when he's mad
at Mis' Royster."

"There's another story only half told.   My friend,
the editor of the *Elk Bend Sharpshooter* says the
secret of good composition is in the suggesting of
more than you really say.   Now, any thoughtful
person could plainly see that Adam's mouth was
watering for that apple all the while, but he didn't dare
touch it.   It was the same spirit which prompts fool-
ishly fond wives of to-day to sneak half the dainties
from their own plate to that of their husband, which
made Eve pick the fruit.   She just couldn't bear to
see his mouth water, and for that she's blamed to this
day.   I always felt lenient towards Eve for another
reason.   She just gave him plain unvarnished apple,
fresh from the tree.   If she'd gone and pealed it, and
mixed up some crust, and baked it, and come to her
lord and master with a specimen of young housekeeper's pie in her hand, I wouldn't venture to take
her part.   Eve was more sensible than ungrateful man
gives her credit for.''

"Mis' Royster says the devil is seekin' to devour all such youngsters as me," suggested Nana.

"Pshaw! You're not at all suitable to the old fellow's taste."

"She said he'd roast me over a fire.   Has he got a fire?"

"Yes, of course.   Raw meat isn't good eating."

"Where do they get their kindlin's?"

"Why bless you, right here where we get ours. They know a thing or two, and one thing they know is that dried sunflower stalks are the very best kindling in the world.   Why, I've seen them skylarking about on this very dairy farm, whisking their tails to keep off the flies, and gathering sunflowers by the armful. They are all black, my children, with long hair and horns.   I fell in with the captain of the band one day, and we sat down and had quite a chat."

"Wasn't you afraid?"

"No, the heart of the virtuous knows no fear."

"Why didn't I ever see him?   I always pull my sunbonnet over my ears and eyes, and run as fast as I can whenever I pass a cornfield, for Bub Royster says he's apt to rush out and catch me any day."

"Ho!   He's too much of a gentleman to do that. He'll leave sneaking ways to Bub Royster and his like.   In fact he said as much to me.   And moreover, he said, 'Mr. Fielding,' he always addressed me as Mr., he was so polite; 'Mr. Fielding,' said he, 'I want to tell you something in strict confidence.   I have an eye to business though I do seem gay and

festive now. I've been thinking pretty hard about
that Royster family up there on the dairy farm.   I
have been wondering for a long time if I hadn't better
bag them, but I can't make up my mind.   The fact
is, Mr. Fielding, (do not mention it, for if it should
get abroad 'twould ruin my reputation forever,) I am
half afraid of them, they are so much worse than I
am.' And the father of darkness actually blushed—
blushed, mind you, and hid his face in his bandana.''

While he was finishing his peculiar little tale, a
young lady mounted on a gentle looking mustang
rode up and joined the company.   So engrossed were
Lucky and the children that they became aware of her
presence only when she spoke.

''My dear Lucky! What nonsense to be giving
those poor, credulous children!''

Lucky looked half guilty, half amused. Taking
off his hat he bowed to the beautiful creature and
muttered something about stating the case as it stood.

''As it stands in your imagination,'' was the gay
reply.   '' Don't mind him, my dears, he isn't truthful.
He is a bad boy. He ran away from home this
morning to escape a disagreeable duty, and I'll tell
you about it.   One day he hired to a certain Mr.
Slocum to do some breaking, but my fastidious
brother, not liking that gentleman's cooking—I
believe he is his own housekeeper—played hooky, and
vowed he'd never go back again. This morning as
his employer came to see about it, the brave young
man shouldered his gun, and escaped through the

back window as Mr. S. entered the front door.   Now shame him."

"I'm not to blame now, am I?" said Lucky. "Everybody knows that Slocum first kneads his bread, then sets it under the stove for the pussy cat to sleep in.   Why, when the bread comes upon the table it is furnished with such a nice set of furs that it is hard to tell where cat leaves off and bread begins."

"I don't believe you, Lucky," said his sister.

"Can't help it.   Have given you the gospel truth as did the prophets before me, and if you don't accept it 'tisn't my fault.   I've done my duty."

Both Miss Fielding and her brother laughed heartily at this, and Lund could not help smiling from sympathy. But Nana's countenance did not change.

"Why so sober, little one?" asked the lady.

"She is thinking of the Great Terrible," said Lucky.

"Come, cheer up, you little wild elfin.   There is not a word of truth in these stories."

"Pooh! I don't care for that," returned Nana, "I've things to bother me that no one knows."

Lucky and his sister smiled again, thinking this speech caught from her elders.

"What is the trouble, little witch?   Has your doll broken its head?" asked Miss Fielding.

"I don't have a doll," answered Nana.

"Indeed! wouldn't you like to have one?"

"No, I'd rather have a almanick."

"Why?" again asked the young lady wonderingly.

" Because it is nice to read."

" Then you can read?"

" Yes. I went to school a term once."

" And you love to read?"

" I should say so. It's my only fun. But I have
to hide to do it."

Having promised to bring the child a whole armful
of story books at no late date, Miss Fielding and her
brother turned to go.

"What an odd child," mused Miss Fielding.

"A regular sprite," said Lucky. "Her name is
Nana, the boy tells me; I've seen him often before,
you know. By the way, that chap will inherit the
earth some day—six feet of it. He's as blindly meek
as an ox. Isn't Nana an odd name for a girl brought
up by the Roysters?"

"Yes, so soft and refined. She's a remarkably
graceful child and more than pretty. They ought to
be proud of her."

"Why bless you she's not a Royster! She's a
child they're just keeping for some reason or other.
How her eyes did open when I told her I had a
personal acquaintance with old Hornie! A Royster
wouldn't have flinched—they are distant connections
of his, you know. Bub is a family name. It's
shortened from Beelzebub."

"Lucky, do learn to curb your imagination a trifle
at least. Do you know, you are getting quite a
reputation in the settlement for that sort of thing?"

"What! Wouldst rob thy gentle brother of his
only joy?"

"Nonsense!"

"Not at all. I like to lie. I believe I have a talent for it. We must cultivate our talents. Everybody says we must."

"Well, the consequences be upon your own head."

"I have often thought of reforming. I will reform, sis, now see if I don't, just to please you. But it is a great sacrifice. You remember the story of the sick lady who died when her looking-glass was broken, because it was all she had to live on. Now what if——"

"Well, there's oats in the bin worth thirty dollars, and we can have a pretty respectable funeral in these parts for that amount. Hadn't we better step up a bit? It is almost noon."

When the Fieldings had passed out of sight, Lund and Nana, who had been watching them eagerly, turned and looked at each other.

"The new neighbors," said Nana.

"Yes, over in the new house. Mis' Royster says they're awfully stuck up. I've seen the feller before, but not the girl. They've only been here two months. She's the one somebody—they think it was Bub Royster—tried to rob one night when she was ridin' home a horseback."

"I remember," said Nana.

"She's as pretty as a picture," said Lund. "But look, Nane, at them cows away off there. Good-bye."

Lund mounted his horse, which was grazing quietly near, and was gone.

Nana went back to the pools where her ducks were

sporting, to dream away the remaining hours of the forenoon. Her mind was full of the new neighbors. She wondered when she would see them again, and what they would say to her.

CHAPTER IV.

BUB AND ROSE.

"ONE of Royster's steers is mired !" shouted Joe Slocum one chilly spring day, darting into the yard of Farmer Dolby on his wiry little mustang.

"Sakes alive !" exclaimed a rosy young girl, who stood in front of the house, scattering crumbs of corn bread to a crowd of noisy fowls which surrounded her. "How did it happen? Ma, hear that ! One of Royster's steers is mired ! Get your bonnet, and come quick !"

"The men folks aint to home," said Mrs. Dolby, bustling out upon the scene with a shawl and hood in her hand. "They have gone to mill, but me and Rose will go over."

"So the men folks aint to home. Then I must look otherwheres for help. But you and Rose go on as you say. Down at the North Pond, mind you. Mis' Royster and Mis' Blake and the gals be all there. Bub and his pa be there too, I guess." This with a side glance at Rose.

The miring of an animal was quite a social event in these regions. It was all that balls, receptions, and races are to their city cousins. So, when Mrs. Dolby and her daughter arrived at the pond, they found a very sociable group gathered on its banks. I do not mean to say they enjoyed the discomfort of the poor brute who stood knee deep in the soft mud, from which he could not extricate himself; but when such circumstances occurred, they made the best of them.

" Them awful sink holes !" exclaimed Rose Dolby. Her gladness of the event which was to bring her in contact with the one she admired above all others, did not obliterate her pity for the unfortunate animal. Her cheeks burned with a ruddy glow, and her pretty lids were becomingly dewy, when Bub arrived. She was the first object his eyes fell upon, and his rough heart gave a quick, jerky thump under his brown ducking jacket. No matter how cruel and unrelenting a man may be, he likes a soft-hearted woman ; and Rose was a perfect picture of sweet sympathy.

Bub's face gave no sign as he looked at Rose. He thought sentiment weak, and his highest ambition was to be considered strong. So he nodded a careless good morning to the girl he loved; then, divesting himself of shoes and stockings, waded out into the water, and proceeded to fasten the ends of an impromptu pulley round the body of the ox, and throw a blanket over its quaking hulk.

" Look out for sink holes, Bub!" shouted the crowd on the bank.

" Yep," responded Bub with a nonchalant shrug.

Rose thought how brave and strong her lover looked, and glowed with fond pride. Her heart yearned towards him; but he was so cold, so indifferent. Would he never change? She was certain that she should never marry if he did not, but remain true to him until death. Rose Dolby's was a firm, loyal heart. Bub was not worthy of such pure and gentle affection; but worth does not always command love. and the unworthy are often thrice blessed in this respect.

"Poor thing! See it shake!" cried a woman in a cracked, disagreeable voice, husky with a cold.

Rose hid her face in her mother's shawl to shut out the sight of the quivering animal. There was a clank of chains and a shout from Bub. He had come ashore and was fastening the other end of the pulley to a pair of whiffletrees. This task was done, the horses were started up, and the ox with groans and struggles, was slowly dragged through the sticky mud and up the steep bank.

Mrs. Royster's grim features relaxed a trifle when she saw the wet, bedraggled condition of her son.

"Go to the house and dry your clothes, child," she advised in tones that were almost caressing.

"Oh bother!" Bub returned savagely shaking off the hand she laid on his arm. He felt that Rose was looking, and he must not display any unmanly weakness. "I've got to run him up and down once or twice, or he'll die. It's only half to get him out."

"But you are wet through. Do go," pleaded Rose softly in his ear. "You'll catch your death of cold."

Bub blushed crimson, and his heart beat wildly again. Her interest in his welfare was very sweet to him, but he would not for the world have shown it. With a harsh, cynical laugh that sent poor Rose trembling and disconsolate back to her mother's side, he muttered something about women's being such geese, and was off at the heels of the martyred ox.

The rest of the party adjourned to the house to drink tea, and gossip for the remainder of the day. Rose was in ecstacy.   To be near Bub for a space of five hours was a rare privilege; and after he had shown himself so heroic too! Love exaggerates virtue in the beloved.   Rose was ready to declare in her heart that Bub was equal to any hero named in history.

Of course, she must be contented to see and admire at a distance, for he would scarcely look at her.   He would play checkers with the men, and talk about pigs and crops.   But what matter ?   She would be near him, she could hear his voice, every slide and trick of which she knew and loved; she could see the motions of his head as it nodded or shook under his sombrero.   How cunning was that movement of the head peculiar to him alone, and how gracefully he spat during the lapses in conversation!   No other man spat like that.

Mrs. Royster came up to introduce Mrs. Blake. Rose bowed absently.   Her thoughts were all on Bub.

" I know Miss Dolby," said Mrs. Blake.   " She got a guinea of me once."

"Oh, did you know her ?   I had no idee you was acquainted," said Mrs. Royster.

"How is the guinea ?" Mrs. Blake asked.

"Pretty well, thank—that is," stammered Rose, "he's dead."

"Oh!" gasped Mrs. Blake with as much feeling as ordinary persons display on hearing of the decease of an acquaintance. "Is that so? How did it happen? Do tell."

"I think the pigs—no, no, I guess a chunk of drift-wood fell on him."

"That Dolby girl is slow, aint she?" remarked Mrs. Blake to Mrs. Royster later on.

"Slow! Law, no! As bright and likely a girl as you ever met. She can wash and iron and sew beautiful, and she makes the best bread and butter in the neighborhood. Besides, she'll have money one of these days. I think my Bub's fond of her," and Mrs. Royster folded her arms and smiled significantly.

After dinner, the men went out to inspect a new blooded calf that Mr. Royster had just bought, while the women washed the dishes and swept. Rose Dolby, catching sight of Nana serenely discussing a basin of corn bread and milk in a corner, sat down by the child, and began to talk. This was the only society a full heart like hers could trust. She was eager to utter the name of her beloved, and Nana she thought, was too young to guess her secret from her conversation. She plied the child with questions about Mrs. Royster, the farm and its appointments; then, tremblingly, she spoke of Bub. Bub—what a strong, manly name! How expressive of the nobility of him who bore it! Rose had whispered it again and again to herself, but to speak it aloud, and listen to the music of it was pleasure unmeasureable.

"Did you see your brother, Bub, when he waded out into the deep, cold wa'er?" queried Rose. "I was so afraid he'd slip and fall."

Nana laughed. That any one should care if misfortune did come to Bub was ludicrous in the extreme. She should have been delighted.

"He aint my brother," was her laconic reply.

"But you love him just as if he were, don't you?"

"No, I don't. Nobody loves Bub Royster."

Rose gave a little start. She was about to protest that she did most truly, but recollected herself in time to check her folly.

"He aint so nice as Lucky Fielding," Nana went on.

"Lucky Fielding! Why he lies and lies and lies. Bub don't."

"Maybe he don't. But I like Lucky. He's good."

"Bub don't like him."

"I don't care. If he don't he needn't."

"But you ought to care. You ought to like Bub. Bub's folks give you a home and clothes to wear and things to eat."

Rose, as many others so often do, had forgotten that love is not a negotiable commodity.

"But Lucky gives me books," said Nana.

"Books! Would you rather have books than a home?"

Nana thought a moment, then replied,

"I couldn't get along without them books. No I couldn't."

" Do you ever expect to fall in love, Nana ? "

Nana nodded promptly. The child had her dreams of the inevitable prince, who would awaken her slumbering heart with a kiss.

" Then, your lover will be brave like my—like Bub, and handsome too like him."

" No, I'm goin' to marry a man like the prince in the Cinderella book Lucky gave me—or else Lucky himself."

Thus the conversation continued till Mrs. Royster seeing Nana idle, a thing she could not bear, sent the child out to gather in chips.

" The little imp has been a worryin' of you," she said to Rose.

" No, no," said Rose who was sincerely sorry that she was gone, "she's a nice child. I am real fond of her."

" She don't improve on acquaintance," said Mrs. Royster sourly. "Since she's got in with them Fieldin's, she's a good deal worse than she used to be."

" How, Mrs. Royster? I heard her say she liked the Fieldings."

" Well, they're a bad, stuck up set. They put her up to all kinds of tricks and spoil her. They would Lund, too, only he's slow. They hate Bub."

" I used to like them myself," said the girl, but I'd no idea they was that kind of folks. I hate them now."

Mrs. Royster went back to her work with a satisfied

smile. It was pleasant to have the prospective heiress agree with her so readily.

The real cause of the feud between Royster and Fielding was this: Miss Fielding, who taught school in an adjoining district, was riding home one evening just at dusk, with the wages for a month's work in her pocket. As she passed a dense corn-field a man with a handkerchief over his face, darted out, and catching her bridle, demanded the money she carried. The brave girl neither screamed nor fainted, but to the utter surprise of the agressor, braced herself in her saddle, and laid her whip about his head in so vigorous a manner, that he soon relinquished his hold and slunk back under the shelter of the corn. The next day, Bub Royster had appeared with face strangely scarred and battered. On being questioned concerning his mishap, he became red and angry, and refused to answer. This had led all to suppose that he was the culprit, and friendly relations between the two families at once ceased.

Evening came. The guests had departed at last, the farm hands had retired, and the Roysters, mother and son, were alone together, save for Nana, who was trying to read by the dim light of a green cottonwood fire.

"See here, young one," growled Bub, "You'd better go to bed. You're not worth your salt since the Fielding's commenced to lend you books. I'll pitch them into the fire first thing you know."

"Don't you dare!" cried Nana glowering upon him.

"Don't talk that way to me."

"I'll do as I please.   I'm not the Dolby girl.   She thinks your an angel, but I don't."

Bub was mollified.   His tones softened.

"How do you know she thinks it?"

"Oh, she's always talking about you; says your brave and strong and handsome.   Guess her eyesight ain't very good."

With this taunt Nana gathered up her books and marched scornfully away.

The remaining two looked at each other for a moment.   Each glowed with pleasure, the one, however, somewhat shamefacedly.   At length, the mother broke the silence.

"There, Bub Royster, if you let the grass grow under your feet before you've asked her, you're a coward and a fool.   She'll have money, some day, and she'll be a tip-top manager."

Bub growled out something about not wanting to be saddled with a wife, but secretely resolved to act upon her advice.

A few days later an opportunity presented itself, and the deed was done.   Bub, the brave, the handsome, the manly was accepted with tears of love and gratitude.

Bub was amazed.

"Don't see what you're cryin' about," he observed sheepishly.

"Oh, Bub, I am so ha-ha-happy!" sobbed Rose throwing herself upon his breast.

Bub swore inwardly and wished he was a thousand

miles away; Rose was a nice girl and was going to
have money, but why need she make such a fool of
herself?

"Kiss me," gasped the sweet tearful bride-elect
clinging to him with moist red lips upturned.

"Lord, what next?" was the inward comment of
the lover who stood awkwardly, hands in pockets,
looking down upon her, but never offering to bestow
the longed for caress.

"Bub, Bub," she pleaded frantically, "why don't
you kiss me? Engaged folks always kiss."

"The deuce, they do!" muttered Bub under his
breath; but what could he do? Rose hung upon his
neck, her lips were within an inch of his, and her eyes
were full of mingled beseeching and perplexity.

Bub struggled with himself a moment, then resolved
that since it must be done, it would be better to have
it over as soon as possible, and stooping gingerly to
the pleading lips, he kissed them, resuming his former
position with the air of a man who had done his duty
and found it not so bad after all.

Yes, Rose was a nice little girl. He felt quite satisfied with himself and her, and actually gave her plump
little hand an approving squeeze, to which she responded with smiles and tears commingled, nestling
close to his side meanwhile, and hiding her blushes in
his waist coat.

But what have philosophers said about the course of
true love? Theirs did not run more smoothly than the
rest. Mr. Dolby was willing to neighbor with the

Roysters, buy of them, sell to them, be civil to them at all times, but when it came to a question of family alliance, he firmly drew the line. Rose should never marry Bub with his consent. He had no use for the fellow.

Mr. Dolby was a good father, and Rose was a dutiful daughter; so she informed her betrothed that they must wait.

"Try to show him your worth, Bub," was her womanly advice.

"He won't give in," was Bub's reply. "We'll have to wait till he dies, and he's liable to outlive us both."

"Then, we won't be married at all," said Rose with dignity. "I must mind my father."

Strangely enough Bub did not become angry at the firm stand Rose had taken. Now that she stood a little beyond his reach, he began to prize her more, and resolved to wait for her, come what might. This resolution was probably the noblest sentiment that had ever stirred his heart. It was Bub's first step towards real manhood.

* * * * * *

A strange thing had occurred. Mrs. Royster had seen a ghost. The appearance, she said, was that of a man, dressed in black broadcloth, riding in a phaeton, drawn by a white horse. Had it simply passed and gone on its way, she would not have thought it odd in the least, but she saw it driving by again and again, with its eyes fixed intently on the house.

Many were the conjectures concerning the mysterious occupant of the phæton. The farm hands were of the opinion that Mrs. Royster had doubled the strength of her habitual nightcap, and Lucky Fielding was heard to remark irreverently that any ghost who would hang around the Royster premises, when he might be haunting a better place with very little inconvenience to himself, showed pretty poor taste, and was not deserving of an honest man's faith.

But ghost or not, the next evening, Mr. Royster lay on a bed of sickness, suddenly and mysteriously stricken down. The doctor was summoned, but came too late.

"Mother—Bub," gasped the dying man. "Mother —Bub—I'm goin'—I'm goin' shore. I've been a bad man, but I want you to do better. I want you to make it all right with little Nane."

With these words, he died. The doctor took his fingers from the still pulse, named the disease to eager inquirers, and went home. Those who looked, declared afterwards that he rode in a phæton and drove a white horse. This explained to their minds quite satisfactorily the mystery of the ghost, and every one was frowned down who dared suggest that it only "happened so."

CHAPTER V.

AFTER FOUR YEARS.

"HULLO, Captain!"

The man who spoke was tall and brawny, with a sharp, though not unkindly eye. He was bending over a rude fire by the roadside, and the light fell upon his shaggy, unkempt hair and rough, travel-stained garments, revealing a story that one could read at a glance. His lot, notwithstanding his rollicking songs about the freedom and joy of a teamster's life, was not one of mild sunshine. Scorching heat, dust storms, rains, long prayed for and cursed for coming, had for many years had their way with this broad shouldered, burly king of the road. The voice of the man was in keeping with his appearance, deep, vital, and with a ring of good fellowship in it that Lund could not resist.

"Hullo, Captain! What do you know?"

It was the time-honored greeting of the teamster. Lund responded half-heartedly, as he pulled his sombrero further over his eyes, and sat down upon the grass. He had grown to be a tall young man. His limbs were lank and bony, and a deep shade of melancholy had settled upon his face.

The teamster placed a soot-covered coffee-pot over the fire, then turned to fish out from a conglomeration

of traps, a small griddle which soon took its place
beside the coffee-pot.

"Get out, Shep!" he cried to the dog at his heels,
which was sniffing at a basin of pancake batter standing
on the ground. "Get out, I say! Here, stranger,
come closer to the light. I want to look at you.
What do you know, anyway? Give us the news."

Lund dragged his awkward body forward in a
spiritless manner, and seated himself anew. His
attitude was one of utter despondence. He sat very
still, watching with dull interest his new acquaintance
spreading pancake batter over the smoking hot griddle.

Far off on either side stretched the rolling prairie,
the lonely monotony of which was unrelieved except
by here and there a grove of cottonwood trees, marking
the location of some farm house, or a clump of alders
surrounding an isolated pool. The teamster's fire
flickered dimly in the twilight. The great, black
snake-like road wound away and away to the west;
the wagon stood beside it with the ox yoke leaning
against the side, and the oxen grazing hard by. It
was a rudely romantic picture.

The low wailing cry of a whip-poor-will broke the
silence.

"Confound the bird!" the teamster exclaimed. "I
wish it'd have the decency to shut up. Makes me feel
as if the whole world had turned into a graveyard. Is
that what ails you, friend?"

Lund shook his head.

"Then what is it? Something's up. Here you,

Shep, you ugly man's cur, keep your nose away from them flippers. You'd better tell me. I've helped many a better and many a worse man, I dare say, out of the dumps."

Lund leaned his head on his hands and the tears rolled down through his gaunt fingers. He was ashamed to shed them, but they must come.

"See here, now," said the teamster kindly, "you are in a peck o' trouble, and I know'd it as soon as I set eyes on you. But if you won't tell a feller, what can a feller do? Is it a girl?"

Lund gave his head another negative twist.

"Is it money?"

The same response.

"Well, then, I swear I can't guess. You don't look old enough to have a mother-in-law."

This was said with so comic a quirk of the lips, that Lund's gravity gave way, and he laughed aloud.

"That's right! That's what I like to hear! It sounds as if there was hopes of heaven for you in the long run," said the teamster. "Go ahead. I'm a listenin'."

Thus enticed out of his reticent mood, Lund opened his heart to his newly found friend. He told how he had that morning been derided by Bub Royster, who was out of humor and spoiling for a fuss, and how finally, because he would not reply to the taunts of his tormentor, he had been knocked down with a pitchfork handle, and after that, had not gone near the house, but had wandered about over the prairie, trying

to think what was best to do.   He did not wish to
return, not because of fear but because he disliked living in continual contention.

"By the old Harry!" swore the teamster mildly,
"I never heard of such a heathen this side of Idaho,
or th' other side neither.   Look here, my boy," slapping Lund's ragged knee, "don't you be down in the
mouth.   I'll take you to Omaha with me, and get you
the best job o' teamin' that's goin'.   My wife'll be a
sister to you.   She'll wash and patch your clothes and
do it cheerfully, sir.   Here's the chance of your life.
Only say the word, and it's a go."

"I'll think about it, and tell you in the morning,"
said Lund.

The teamster's supper was shared with his visitor,
and after it was eaten, the man said:

"Well, you'd better bunk with me to-night.   I'm
glad of your company.   Company is a powerful anec-
dote for the blues.   Now I'll make the bed, and we'll
turn in, for I'm as tired as a nigger."

The bed was not much to make.   There were only
a few blankets to spread out on the ground under the
wagon.   The two retired, and the teamster was soon
asleep; but the young man at his side lay awake, watching the smouldering coals of the dying fire, the great,
white moon, sailing along in the sky, and the shadows
that rested under the little hills.   The wide expanse of
silent prairie spoke to his heart, telling him a story
which he, rough and unlearned as he was, could not
have embodied in words.   It was his.   It had been his

throughout all his previous life. Others might hold the right and title to those hills and ravines, but there was something in them which no one could take from him, as long as he chose to retain it. He did not know what it was but he felt its power within him.

How he loved the loneliness and grandeur! How his spirit sank when he thought of leaving it forever! Ginger, the pony must have a new rider, and the little spiked horn heifer and her companions must find a new friend.

The grass stirred gently about his bed, the dog snoozed peacefully, dreaming of rabbit hunts, with now and then a soft, delighted bark, a charred stick burned off at one end, and fell with a smothered thud into the bed of gray ashes, and the oxen sighed loudly in their sleep.

The moon sank out of sight, and still Lund lay awake, under the broad blue of the sky with the little stars looking down at him, thinking of the new life which lay ahead. When he thought of freedom, his heart warmed; but for that freedom he was paying a price.

The fire went out, the stars paled, and it grew quite dark. Yet Lund did not sleep. He was still thinking.

Morning came, breakfast was over, the team was hitched to the wagon, and the driver mounted on his seat.

" Are you comin' ? " he asked turning to Lund.

Lund put his foot on the wheel, ready to mount. A vague light shone in his eyes. It was the light of new hope mingled with a deep shadow of regret. For a moment he stood irresolute; then, his hand dropped from the side-board like lead, and looking wistfully at the teamster he spoke:

"I want to go—the Lord only knows how I want to go—but I cant leave Nane—little Nane."

"Well, I'm sorry," the teamster replied; "there was the makin' of a man in you."

But he had no time to argue the case. He cracked his whip, shouted to his oxen, and the wagon began to move, the dog bounding along ahead.

Lund stood and looked after the moving team until it was almost out of sight. There was a great lump in his throat, and the ground seemed to reel beneath his feet.

The wagon had reached the top of the hill. The driver turning round, waved his hat as a parting salute. Lund answered with a feeble gesture of the hand, then turned sorrowfully to go back to the Roysters' and take up his cross again.

*   *   *   *   *   *   *

"Nana, Nana!" called Mrs. Royster to the girl who was tripping down the path, which led to the north of the house, and was already several yards away. "Nana, where are you goin', child?"

"To the North Pond to gather sunflowers."

"Pshaw! What do you want of them weeds?"

"I like them."

"Well, the Dolbys have just brought home a new

Texas steer, so you'd best be careful. He might get away," warned Mrs. Royster."

" I am not afraid."

" So it seems about other things as well as this. But you'd best listen to them that's older than you. In my time, young folks used to pay some attention to their elders, but it 'pears that time's gone past — with some anyway."

Nana paid little heed to Mrs. Royster's words of complaint as she no longer feared the woman. She had been treated more kindly since the death of Mr. Royster. Either his dying words or Joe Slocum's threats had borne fruit. She had been well clothed and fed and when one day, she announced her intention of starting to school in the district adjoining, where Miss Fielding taught, no one offered to oppose her. She was now sixteen years of age, and competent to take charge of a school herself. Miss Fielding had found in her a remarkable pupil especially in history and literature. She was beautiful too, as well as brilliant, but she was not vain. Her training had not been conducive to vanity.

Mrs. Royster stood with arms akimbo, her eyes bent upon the ground. Suddenly, she raised them, and looking into Nana's face, said in a confidential tone:

"You don't expect to go past the Fieldin's, do you ? "

" Scarcely."

" I wouldn't, Nana."

"Why?   Have they some wild cattle, too?"

"No, but I wouldn't let my head run upon Lucky Fieldin', if I was you, or appear to be lettin' it neither. He's some years older than you, though he does act like a great boy, and he'll only laugh at you for your pains.   Besides, you must remember that though you be so fine, your eddication is all that me and Bub is like ever to give you, as Bub'll be marryin' one of these days, and will want what he has, and Lucky Fieldin' is not the man to take up with a penniless girl."

Nana blushed, as Mrs. Royster's keen eyes searched her face.

"You can't trust him, neither," the woman went on.   "I've heard tell that he's a reg'lar jilt.   The mail carrier told me, and some one told it to him as a pos'tive fact that two summers ago, when he went East, he met a girl that he made love to with all his might, and then left her, and she felt so bad about it that in a month or so after, she died.   The mail carrier says that the woman who told him knew a woman who was a great friend of the girl's."

Mrs. Royster watched Nana out of sight, with something like a smile hovering about her thin lips.   She felt that her arrow had struck home, though the girl had given no sign.

Nana and Lucky since their first meeting had been firm friends.   He had read to her, and had told her of that land of dreams lying beyond the line of hills which hid it from her vision, the great world where men were so brave and gallant, and women so bright and beautiful.

He had made her long for that world, and sometimes there had crept into her heart along with other dreams, the desire that he might one day take her there.　Of late the wish had occurred more frequently, for at times, Mrs. Royster with her nagging, and Bub with his rough ways and uncouth manner, nearly drove her to distraction.　It was but natural that she should think of Lucky.　He always joined her in her walks when his work permitted, and that was often.　He always talked of the things she cared for, and his ways were so different from those of the Roysters.　Now, the words of the woman rankled in her mind.　Was Lucky a jilt?　Was he amusing himself with her, thinking easily to gain her love for the mere pastime of it?　At any rate he should see that it was not so easy a matter to do.　With this resolution firm in her heart she walked along that bright summer morning till she had reached the North Pond, where the tall sunflowers tossed their haloed faces in thick profusion.

Instead of gathering her lap full, as had been her intention, she sat down in the shade to think.　How would it be best to treat Lucky Fielding when next they met?　She had not been sitting there long, when she heard a low fierce bellow not far away.　"The Dolby's steer," was her first thought, and looking up, she saw tearing down the hill, a great angry creature, with wide spreading horns, which he dug into the earth as he bounded on, snorting menacingly.

He had seen her—flight would be worse than useless.　She crouched down among the sunflowers to await her doom. He was upon her now; his horns touched the ground not a foot from where she sat, and his great red eyes looked into hers. She sat so still that the animal seemed perplexed, and offered no further demonstrations, but stood with horns still lowered, watching her. Nana felt that it was only a question of a few moments, nevertheless; she began to repeat her prayers mechanically, as she had learned to do when a child, from an evangelist who had held a revival meeting in the school house.

Presently a rider appeared on the brow of the hill, spurring his horse to its utmost speed. It was Lucky Fielding, and he carried a pitchfork in his hand. He was soon to the rescue. The steer was driven off, and he stood by her side holding her cold hands.

"My eye! but you are a plucky one! Why didn't you screech out and get killed?"

Nana drew her hands away and laughed carelessly. Lucky glanced at her with a disapproving look.

"You can laugh, can you, when you've just come back from death's very door?"

Nana scarcely opened her lips in reply; her words were cold, and only half audible.

"I knew the beast had strayed," Lucky went on. "I was working in the field when Rose came running to me with the news. I thought of you in a minute, you are out on the hills so much, and it did not take me long, I tell you, to unhitch and mount Firefly. I left the other horse in the field, but he'll stand. I'll take you home now."

" I'm not at all afraid. I can go alone."

" And run the risk of meeting Sir Texas again ?"

" He went another direction."

" Then, you don't want my company ?"

" Just as you please."

" Well, I please to go, for there's no telling whether you'll be safe or not. Then I will ride after the old fellow and see that he's put up."

They walked along silently. Lucky began to be nettled by Nana's cool demeanor. He cared for the girl, having for some time looked upon her as his own, and thought she understood it.

" Playing the high and mighty, hey ?" he said to himself, as he saw at length that Nana was not at all disposed to converse. " Well, I'll have my game too. I promised sis not to lie any more, but this once I cannot resist. Let me see, what shall I say ?"

Lucky thought a moment, then began.

" I say, Nana, I've something to tell you. You've always been a good little sister to me, and I feel that I can come to you with all my plans, and receive sympathy and advice. I've been thinking for a long time about getting married. Don't laugh. Every young man thinks of such things. You'll promise you won't laugh if I tell you a secret ?"

Nana promised, with the same coolness of manner.

" Well, to make short work of it, you know that there are no marriageable young ladies about here ex-cept Rose Dolby, and she persists in becoming an old maid for the sake of his lordship, Bub Royster. You,

Nana, are as yet only a child, and besides, I have always looked upon you as a sister. Well, I've made up my mind to start to-morrow for the Upper Missouri, partly to shoot teal and partly to get myself a wife. I hear that a lot of girls have lately arrived at Dannerborg, near the rapids, and the fellows are flocking there from all sections. I think I'll go and see if any of 'em suit my fancy. Romantic—hey sis?"

The falsehood was told calmly, soberly, as only Lucky Fielding could tell it.

"I wish you good luck," Nana answered in a voice not altogether free from sarcasm. "Shall you take time to court her, or just pick her out and marry her off hand?"

"Oh I shall follow the prevailing fashion whatever that may be," Lucky responded. Then he bade her good-bye for they had reached Royster's boundary line over which the Fieldings seldom deigned to step.

Mrs. Royster met Nana as she came wearily up the path to the house. She noted the girl's tired eyes and languid walk.

"Where are your sunflowers?" she asked.

"I did not think of them," Nana returned. "I have just escaped being killed by Dolby's Texas steer."

"Law sakes! You don't say! How did it happen?"

Nana told the story.

"Lucky Fieldin' drove him away!" exclaimed

Mrs. Royster in consternation. "Well, I s'pose you'll be a marryin' him the next thing, won't you?"

"No," Nana answered, "I shall never marry Lucky Fielding."

Mrs. Royster's countenance changed in an instant.

"Well," she said in a conciliatory voice, "Bub calculates goin' to L this week, with a load of cheese, and he spoke of takin' Rose and you along, and he says as you have been a likely girl, I'd best give you a little money to spend while you're there." With this, Mrs. Royster put a twenty-dollar bill into Nana's hand.

"I want you to get yourself a new checkered de-lain, and a pair of pretty slippers with shiny buckles like the mail carrier's wife had on the day she rode here with him, and a new hat, and some pocket hand-kechers, and any other little thing you may want."

Mrs. Royster went into the house, and Nana stood staring after her, wondering at such benevolence.

It was very strange.

CHAPTER VI.

IN THE CITY.

NANA went with the load of cheese to L, Rose Dolby accompanying her. They started a little after midnight, that they might reach the city before the day grew hot. Joe Slocum, wishing to make a few purchases in shape of furniture for his house, went along, as well as Lund who drove the team.

As the way was very dark, a small lantern was swung at the head of either horse; Bub slept with his head on Rose Dolby's lap, Rose and Slocum dozed, while Nana sat wide awake, her back braced against a pile of cheese boxes. The wagon rattled dismally along, and the dreary, continuous tramp of the horses' feet filled her with intense loneliness. She wished that Lund would speak to her, or even turn his head, but he sat stiff and solemn in his seat, giving his attention to the road in front, over which the two lanterns shed a pale light. She was tempted to speak to him; but no, it would do no good. She could not tell him her secret. She must bear her loss and disappointment alone. But it made her more lonely to see him, her only friend, sitting there with his back to her, his slouch hat pulled over his eyes, intent upon his work, and she believed, with no thought beyond it. Thus she sat meditating until many miles lay between her and the Royster farm.

Joe Slocum woke, and looked towards the east.

"Day is breakin'," he remarked.

"How far are we from L?" Nana inquired.

"Near fifteen miles yet. Are you happy, little 'un?"

"As much as usual, thank you," was the dry response.

"Do you know what you're goin' to L for?"

"Yes, to see the city. I've never seen a city."

"You are goin' for sometin' more than that."

"What for?"

"To buy your weddin' clothes."

"Nonsense. I am not going to be married."

"Yes, you air."

"How do you know?"

"Mis' Royster and me have calc'lated on it."

Nana's heart stood still. Nothing had ever been said of her marriage with Joe since the day she and Lund had talked it over on the prairie, the day she had first met Lucky Fielding, and gradually the fear of it had slipped from her mind, as impending calamities that have done no more than threaten, are wont to do. But here it was confronting her again. She controlled herself until she was able to inquire with calmness.

"What do you mean?"

"That you air a goin' to marry me next comin' Wednesday. We'll invite some people, and have a shake-down at the Roysters' to celebrate. You can dance the Diner Polka then to your heart's content. I'll have the fiddlers up from Elk Bend. I know you be fond o' dancin'."

"And I have nothing to say about this, I presume."

"Why, we cal'clated you should be suited. No expense will be spared for the jubilee. You needn't worry your head, little 'un. You'll have nothing to find fault with."

"I do not mean that. I mean that I think you and Mrs. Royster ought to have asked my consent to this arrangement which seems to be a settled matter between me and you."

"Why? Don't you want to get married, gal?"

"No."

"Why? Ain't I always been good to you and saved you from lots o' trouble? Ain't it I that saw to your bein' eddicated? Ain't—"

"Oh yes, Joe, and for that I am grateful. But gratitude is not love."

"Can't you love me a bit, my pretty, if you try real hard?"

"No, Joe. I am sorry, but I never can. You are a man, Joe. You'll let me alone and not plague me any more about it."

"Sorry, little 'un, but I can't let you alone. I've counted on it, year after year, and waited, always a-thinkin' of the happy days a-comin'. I've clinched the bargain with the Roysters, and am a-furnishin'

my house now. Business is business, and love is
another thing. Lettin' love alone, I've done without
a housekeeper five years, waitin' for you, and now,
you mustn't go back on me. You'll have no hard
times, little 'un. You'll not find me a bad man.''

Nana saw that words from her on the subject would
be wasted, so sighed and kept silent. But her thoughts
were busy the remaining fifteen miles of her ride, and
before they reached L. she had made up her mind
what to do.

*   *   *   *   *   *

The long, tiresome day in the hot streets of the city
finally came to an end, and the two girls were closeted
in a little box of a room, under the roof of a small
Dutch hotel, while the men slept in the wagon on the
haymarket square, to guard the produce yet unsold,
and save the price of lodging.

The room was dingy and cheerless, and a smell of
onions pervaded the air. Rose let down her long hair,
and looked at Nana, who sat at the foot of the bed,
nursing her knees in her slender arms.

" Isn't this glorious !'' cried the former young lady.

" I can't say that I see the glory of it,'' Nana
answered.

" Why, we are sleeping all alone in a hotel for the
first time in our lives.''

" And if this is a fair sample of hotels, I hope it will
be the last.''

" Haven't you enjoyed yourself to-day, dear ?''

" No.''

"What! Do you mean to say you don't enjoy looking at pretty things? Why, I should be crazy with joy if I could buy such things as dear Mrs. Royster is giving you. That delaine of yours is just grand! It is pretty enough for a wedding dress."

"It is for my wedding dress, Rose."

Rose looked at her a moment with beaming eyes, then throwing her arms round Nana's neck cried out joyfully:

"Oh, I am so glad! Who is it, dear? Lucky Fielding?"

"No. Lucky Fielding has gone away to the Upper Missouri to shoot teal and get himself a wife."

Rose gave a little gasp of surprise, and took her arms away.

"I can't think who it is, then," she said, knitting her brows in perplexity.

"The last person you'd guess in the world," said Nana, looking at her so intently that Rose sprang up with a little scream.

"Goodness gracious! Not my Bub?"

"Not so bad as that," said Nana, smiling grimly. "You want to know who it is, do you? Well, its no other than Joe Slocum."

Rose's eyes widened till they looked like great, blue saucers.

"You don't say so!"

"Yes, he's the Roysters' choice, not mine. What do you think of him?"

"Well," said Rose consolingly, "he'll be a good

provider, and you'll get used to him after a while."

Nana laughed a quiet laugh of superiority, which nettled Rose, though she did not understand exactly what it meant.

" Oh, I know he isn't a bit like Bub," Rose said.

" No, thank heaven for that."

" You musn't speak so to me !"

" Why, musn't I defend my bridegroom? I thought you were more reasonable. Bub is very fond of you, Rose, and you are a good woman. I hope you'll make a man of him."

" I know you don't like Bub. You misunderstand him. So do pa and ma. Now, I understand him perfectly, and know how good he is at heart," rejoined Rose earnestly.

The girls said no more, but went to bed. Innocent Rose soon slept the sleep of the tired and happy. Not so her companion. For her, the long hours of the night dragged slowly by. Her heart and head were both heavy with weariness and anxiety, but she dared not close her eyes, lest she should oversleep. When the clock in the town hall struck four, she arose and dressed herself quietly, that she might not awaken Rose. Her hasty toilet made, she lifted the latch, hurried down the rickety stair, unbolted the street door, and stepped out into the misty gray of the morning.

She passed the wagon in the hay market where her associates slept, and hastened on through the unfamiliar streets. Her object was to lose herself from her companions till it should be safe to do more. When the sun came up, she was far away from the little Dutch hotel.

She had reached the suburbs of the city. Perceiving a great building, evidently a church, with a wide portico, she conceived the idea of sheltering herself beneath it for a time, that she might rest. To her surprise and delight, she found the door ajar, and into the quiet vestibule she crept with a sweet sense of safety and protection, as if God had opened His arms to her in her hour of trouble. Tired out from the long walk, she lay down on one of the cushioned pews, and fell asleep.

Some hours after, she was awakened by a gentle touch on her forehead. Opening her eyes, she saw bending over her, a silver-haired old man, dressed in long, black robes. The tenderness of his voice and eye inspired her at once with implicit confidence.

" Well, my stray lamb ?" was his greeting.

"I was tired and came in here to rest," Nana explained apologetically.

" Ah yes, ah yes. May God bless you. There is no better rest than that which is found in the house of the Lord. You have found out the true secret of life, my child. You have flown for your rest to the feet of the Lord."

He waited for an answer, but receiving none he continued,

"You have come a long way. Your shoes and dress are dusty. May I know your errand in these parts ? "

" It may not be in these parts," Nana answered. "I am looking for Dr. Eustace, the wealthy gentleman, who does so much charitable work."

" Dr. Eustace—Dr. Eustace," mused the priest. "The name is not familiar to me. Do you know the street and number? If not, we must look for it in a directory."

Nana knew the street and number. She knew the story on the paper she had treasured to that day, by head and heart. Only her love for Lucky had kept her from writing to the good and wealthy man, asking him to do something toward her education. Lucky and Lucky only had held her to the dairy farm. Now that he was gone, there was no use in trying to remain, even if the Roysters did not intend to compel her to marry Joe Slocum.

" The address is No. 7 M Street," said Nana.

" Ah yes. That will not be difficult to find. I will send one to guide you by and by. In the meantime, come to my house, which is near at hand, and receive the material food that we as agents of the Lord are commanded to administer as well as spiritual nourishment. You shall be waited upon by my niece, a good lady, who likes little girls."

With these words, he took her by the hand, and led her as he would a child, into the parsonage.

Later in the day, she stood at the door of No 7 M Street, and knocked. The house was not a prepossessing structure nor was it in a very handsome quarter. Nana thought at first that she must have made a mistake; but no, there was the number above the door. Then she reflected that the benevolent gentleman who lived to do good to others probably gave away so much that he had little for himself. The shutters rattled dismally in the wind as she stood waiting. No one came to the door. She knocked again.

There was a shuffling of slipshod feet within, and a grumbling voice was saying something about folks who didn't know enough to ring the bell, after which the door opened, and the shocky head of an Irish woman was poked out.

"I wish to see Dr. Eustace," Nana faltered. "Is this his house, and is he in?"

"Och! Now, I guess you be after manin' me b'y, Stacy. Come in. What be ailin' ye, my pretty?"

"Nothing. I wanted to see the doctor," said Nana with sinking heart.

The Irish woman led her into a disorderly room, and opening a stair door at the left, called hoarsely,

"Stacy! Stacy!"

There was no response.

"Stacy, ye dumb lune, be after stirrin' your stumps. There's a lady here to see ye and very ill she is."

There was a scuffing of feet above, and soon some one began to descend the stairs.

Poor Nana! The man who appeared before her was not the Dr. Eustace of her dreams.

He was short and thick set with red face and shocky hair like his mother's, but he looked good natured and even kind.

" And is it me ye be afther wishin' to consult?" he inquired in a rich brogue, as he stooped to examine Nana's pulse.

" I want to see Dr. Eustace, but I'm not sick at all!" Nana blurted out.

"Och!" grunted the mother, " It's crazy the poor child is! I was after seein' it in her eye from the firrust."

" I am Docther Eustace at your sarvice, mum," said the man with a bow.

You are not the Dr. Eustace who builds schools— you are not this Dr. Eustace?" and Nana drew from her little purse, a crumpled wood cut which she had clipped from the paper the teamster had given her long ago.

The doctor examined it with chuckles of admiration.

" That's me! I'm your identical huckleberry!" he cried at last. "Sure and ye've not missed your mark, whin ye aimed here. I niver founded a school, bejab- bers, but doesn't the proverb say thot the intintion is as good as the dade? Faith, and I would have been born handsome too, like thot, if sarcumstances had not been ag'inst me. I didn't have me own way about thot at all, at all, but is not the intintion as good as the dade? What is your business wid me, missy?"

Nana tired and sick at heart, unable to bear her disappointment longer, burst into tears.

"Och, now, acushla! Don't be after a doin' av thot! What be ailin' ye? If ye be in nade av a frind, Stacy Bond's your b'y!"

He was touched by her distress and strange beauty. He declared that he was willing to lay down his life for her if necessary, and when the whole of the sad story was drawn from the reluctant lips of the runaway, he exclaimed, slapping his salt and pepper trousers in real delight.

"Faith, and ye did roight me plucky darlint, and Stacy Bond's the b'y that'll stand by ye through foire and water, through thick and thin!"

CHAPTER VII.

A PROPOSAL.

STACY BOND was Dr. Eustace Bond, better known to consumers of patent medicine as Dr. Eustace. He related the story of his start in life to Nana thus :

" The poit says thot tongue is long and toime is fleetin', but as nayther you nor I seems pressed wid business, ye might loike to hear how such a homely man as me can take so foine a photygraph. I tuk it from the counter av a protygraph store, begarry, or I shouldn't have had it, nayther. The man whose loikness it was had gone to the Californy shore, and I knew 'twas safe, for if Dr. Eustace's rimidies should travel thot fur,'twould make me rich enough to convince any coort thot he had stolen me countenance instid av I his loikness. I hoired a man to wroite me touchin' stories fer the papers. Thot was some toime afther I firrust went into business, howsomever.

" I was but a orphint mesel' and me mither a widdy, and the workhouse a stretchin' out its yearnin' arrums fur us both. The poit Spearshook says ' How sublime a thing it is to suffer and growl it out, begarry ; ' but Stacy Bond did not agree wid the ould spalpeen. I resolved mesel' to stir me stumps and chate bad fortune. I obeyed the sage dictates av me conscience which said to me, said it ' Stacy Bond, me b'y, ye want bread, and if I'm not mistook your principles be not agin the havin' av your bread buttered, wid ever and anon, a relish av beefsteak and froid onions. Ye have often been told by your rich and distant—ahem—relations thot no b'y should have tastes above his station. So if ye can't suit your stummick to your station, Stacy, me b'y, ye must suit your station to your stummick. Ye are fond of hoigh art, especially in the desoigns av meat poys and sich artistic cupboard furniture and break-your-back. Ye know thot a thing av beauty is a j'y forever, as well as the poit did whin he said so, and ye know thot there's nothin' more beautiful than a dish av roast pig wid parsely av a Thanksgivin' Day.

"Ye know what ye want, your rich uncles and aunts, nivertheless. Ye don't hanker for gems thot glisten wid financial loight, ye are not at present a chasin' afther the broight feathered and fleet winged birrud called fame ; but ye do pine fur a square meal three toimes a day, even if the feelin' don't quoite coincoide wid the rules av political economy. Let Sokratix prate and Salamander argy, the lariat av Tinnyson is not to be compared wid a good dinner. A good dinner has more enloightenment in it than a whole art loan crammed wid Purillos and Raffles. It breathes out an eddicative influence thot knocks to smithereens all the tenets av Mill and Spincer.

"This was my philosophy. I soon started down the strate wid a satchel slung over me back forhinst me. It wa'n't no arishtocratic, upper crust av a satchel, nayther ; but if patches is respictable, as they says they is, then thot same trusty carpet bag had plenty av roight to respict. I can't say much fer the halin' power av its inner contents. I made it mesel' out av sugar and flour wid a little Queen Ann mixed in to give it a mediciny flavor to plaze the popular taste.

"I felt aisy in me mind fer me rimidies was as good as any av the kind in the market. Who expects to gather paches from a thistle crop, or to get a whole system full av good health from a patent medicine bottle? But there was another thing thot troubled me soul and very near broke me back. The satchel was heavy wid its weight of rimidies fer every disaise known to mortal man, as Shokespook says; then I said to mesel', 'Now, Stacy, ye crazy lune, bad luck to ye, why don't ye invint a rimidy thot will cure all disaises to wanst?' That I did, and whin next I shinned it down the strate, I carried wid me a rimidy thot would knock anything to flinders from a pin prick av a pain in the left corner av the north east eye to a broken limb av three months' standin'. Faith and St. Patrick, it was a rimidy! 'Twas thot which made me fortune.

"Whin firrsut I started me men in the field, I had crazy work av it, fer oftentoimes they trisspassed on each others torryterry, and then there was war to the broom-schtick handle. The ladies who had seen wan av me agents were not anxious to pursue the acquaintance av another unless wid a butcher knoif. 'Twas an evil day fer me, begarry. So says I to me inmost soul, 'Stacy, me b'y, ye've got your thinkin' cap on the wrong soide av your head. Rouse up and straighten it, or ye're a

ruined man.' The result av me miditation was that
whin next I sallied out, I hugged an idee close to me
throbbin' breast.

"I rung a bell, and the misses appeared, or ruther
the ultimate end av her nose did through an infinitely
small crack in the dure. 'Be off wid ye!' says she,
poloightly.

"'Excuse me kindly, mum,' says I, 'but I have a
missage av importance to give ye.'

"'Come in, thin,' says she.

"The Rubbercorn was crossed whin I crossed the
threshold. Knowin' thot I now had the advantage, I
could be as darin' as plazed me fancy. I drew down
me mug till it closely resimbled a funeral procession on
the Fourth av Juloy, and says I to her, 'Me grand-
mither is dead,' says I.

"'Poor b'y!' says she, in a pityin' tone.

"'That's what I am, and roight ye are in two sinses
av the word,' says I. Then I related in me most heart
crushin' tone the story av the good lady's death.
Thrue, she doied before ever I was born, but what av
thot? A man who would spake av the death av so
near a relative widout the sheddin' av a few tears is a
wretch indade. I did me duty, ye may as well belave.
I stirred her heart, and when I saw it I says, says I,
'But the most terrible part av it is she moight have
been saved.'

"By this toime I was settin' in the parlor on a sofy,
wid a grand pianny at me roight and an illegant mirror
at me left, a sippin a' glass av foine wine, as who would

refuse to do wid a broight and beautiful lady a urgin' him, and a sighin' and sayin' 'Poor b'y !'

" 'Tell me av it,' says she.   I was always a master hand to get on wid the ladies.

" 'That I will,' says I.   'There is nothing in the world so vallyable for influenza, or malariar or any disaise you moight mintion as Dr. Eustace's Miraculous Compound.   This her mourners urged her to take.   But she was orthydox and employed a docther who called himself a regelar, and he declared it was contrary to medical antics to allow her to take a rimidy so newly dishcovered.   So she doied.'

" 'Don't name the name av Dr. Eustace in me prisence,' says she.

" 'Be aisy, ma'am, be aisy!   What have ye agin Dr. Eustace, the blissed man?'

" 'Some man sold me some av his warthless whoite powders,' says she.

" 'Whoite powders?' says I.   'Dr. Eustace sells no whoite powders.'

" 'Do me ears decave me?'

" 'No, mum, ye hear straight,' and I tuk from me faithful satchel some black powders to convence her.

" 'Twas aisy enough to set down me own agents as imposters, and them me the same, savin' our backs many a time from the poker and the rimidy from losin' av its repitation.   Whin our customers had been a buyin' av black powders we gave 'em whoite, and if whoite and black we gave 'em yellow.

" By these manes I was at length able to trade on a

larger scale. I got me stories wrote and printed, and me borryed photygraph fixed at the top. I started all me men out in little wagons, and me rimidy was soon so much in demand thot the drug stores in some places was glad to handle it. I have a winnin' way peculiar to mesel' alone thot gets the hearts av me customers. And now I am gittin' gradually on to fortune.''

Dr. Eustace set Nana to work folding and addressing circulars, and labelling bottles, which he usually hired done when he did not have time to attend to it himself. He paid her a small amount, and his mother was persuaded to throw in board and lodging. It was not an ideal situation, but she resolved in the meantime to be looking for another. In the stories she had read, persons were always on the watch for bright young ladies such as she, to serve as companions, in which situations they were made much of, and finally ended by marrying into the family, *et cetera*. But no one seemed to want Nana. The close of her first month in L. found her still working with circulars and paste.

You have heard Stacy's life history as told by himself; but his mother had a sequel in preparation.

Biddy Pitchly was a laundry girl, and a lady of beauty and wealth. She had a fine presence, weighing nearly two hundred pounds at the lowest, a peach pudding face, sweet as a rose, Mrs. Bond declared, cunning little eyes that you scarcely could see for the plumpness of her cheeks, and round, red arms, strong for loving embraces and the washboard. She dressed elegantly in furbelows of gorgeous colorings. She had a hundred dollars in the bank, and an uncle who could leave her as much more if he would only be accommodating enough to die. She was fond of Stacy, and if he did not return her affection, he was a muttonhead, or so said Mrs. Bond.

Mrs. Bond had never favored Stacy's new help. She saw in Nana a dangerous rival to her favorite. That the girl would not jump at the chance of marrying her idolized son never entered her head.

It was the beginning of Nana's fifth week at the Bonds'. She was busy at her little table in the room which Stacy and his mother dignified by the name of "Office." Her employer entered, and began to compliment her quickness and deftness of hand.

"Faith, I could not do widout ye," he declared.

"Some one else will do as well when I go," laughed Nana.

"You must never go, me darlint," said Stacy.

Nana paid no attention to the affectionate appellation. Stacy and his mother were given to such epithets.

"Me darlint," he said again, as Nana folded her last circular, and having laid it upon the pile at her elbow, arose to go.

Nana started. If there was nothing unusual in his manner of addressing her, there certainly was in the tone.

"Don't be scared, alanna," he continued as he

noticed the change in her face. "A bit av a choild loike ye may not be used to such things, so I will be koind enough to warn ye beforehand. I'm a' goin' to propose."

"To propose!" Nana was utterly astonished.

"Faith yes. And why not? Ain't me business prosperous enough to permit me to have a woife? I've been a thinkin' av it since the day ye firrust came. Says I to mesel', 'Stacy Bond, me b'y, did ye ever see such eyes and such hair? And did ye ever see such a smart girrul, at all, at all? She's just the woife fer ye, Stacy Bond, says I. But be aisy, I'm a goin' to do me courtin' up in schtoile, loike they does in the books, never fear. Angel av me heart, loight av me soul, hallelujah av me eyes—''

Nana's patience gave way. She interrupted him at this juncture with the petulant exclamation:

"Oh, Dr. Eustace, do stop your nonsense!"

"Be aisy, Miss. It may be imbarrisin', but it is essintial. A marriage can not go on widout the preliminaries, at all, at all, so plaze don't interrupt. Sure and I have been a thinkin' av this fer a long toime, and know how to do it. Beauteous wan, have ye never felt in the hivin av me prisence a devoin extatic swellin' av the soul—av the soul—av—av— och! I have fergot me piece, but the long and short av it is, me darlint, though Biddy Pitchly be a wantin' me to have her, I loike ye best, acushla, and I'll have ye if ye'll have me, 'sure as the stump grows round the voine,' as Spokeshear says."

Nana was too angry and distressed to answer, but slipped through the arms that were reached out to clasp her, and hurried to her own room. Sitting down on the floor, she gave vent to her feelings in a loud burst of laughter, half mirthful, half hysterical, after which, she composed herself and put on her hat for her accustomed walk.

As she stepped into the hall, she encountered Mrs. Bond. That lady did not seem to be in the best of humors.

"Sure and what is this ye mane, ye simple little country gawk, a sittin' yoursel' to lure away the tinder affictions av me only son, and he a refoined profissional gintleman?" she burst out.

Nana protested that she had sought to gain the affections of no one.

"Och! Don't I know? Wa'n't I a listenin' wid me own ears at the kayhole? Ye've been a schemin' to outwit his poor ould mither that's spent years a plannin' fer her b'y, and his future."

"You are mistaken, Mrs. Bond. I have tried to outwit no one."

"And ye don't mane to say thot ye hadn't any desoigns on me son?"

"I mean to say just that."

"Ye have, ye little whoite wretch!"

Nana was by this time too indignant to control herself.

"I tell you Mrs. Bond, that you are altogether mistaken. To tell you the whole truth, your son is not the style of man I would care to marry, so you can set your heart at rest."

"Do ye mane to insult me, his own mither? Why me b'y Stacy is good enough for the Quane's daughther, much less than you that he picked up off the strate. Out av me house this minute, ye hussy, and don't step your foot inside me dure agin!"

Nana found herself thrust by strong hands into the street and the door closed behind her.

For a time she walked along undecided. She had no wish to return to the Bonds. Everything about the house was distasteful to her, and now it would be unbearable.

She had gone some distance, when the sign "Employment Bureau" greeted her eyes. A new idea occurred to her. Without hesitation, she mounted the steps and went in. The interior of the room was none too inviting. The walls were bare and the window hangings tattered and dusty. Several chairs were scattered around the place, and five or six coarse-featured women were loitering aimlessly about. Nana held a brief conversation with the woman at the desk, who eyed her disapprovingly.

"There ain't much ever comes along for girls like you," she said. "I s'pose you can't do very hard work. Have you ever lived out?"

"No," Nana faltered.

"There ain't many calls for help that ain't got strength."

"I never was called weak."

The woman looked at her again very closely.

"What would you like to do?"

"I had thought of going as companion to an invalid lady."

"We don't have many such calls, and you'd never stand a house maid's duties. I guess you don't know what's before you. Have you a home?"

"No," said Nana, and a chilly sensation crept over her, as she realized how utterly desolate she was. For the first time since leaving the Royster farm, she wished herself back.

"Well, we'll see, we'll see," said the woman kindly. "There may be a call. We do get one now and then. I'd advise you to register and keep up heart."

Nana registered, and went away feeling that something must come of it. She had been educated in books, and in books, something always happens in the nick of time. The story of utter and continuous failure seldom is told in literature ; it is too uninteresting.

CHAPTER VIII.

THE PALLADIAN ACADEMY AND NEW LESSONS OF LIFE.

AT the small lodging house where Nana had at last found a refuge within her means, she was still waiting. A week had nearly elapsed and nothing had come to her. She was in her room looking over her small belongings which she had hired a boy to fetch from the Bonds', and calculating how long the price of certain articles would keep her alive if sold, in case she found no work. There were only a few books and trinkets of little value indeed. Nana glanced over her shoulder into the small cracked looking-glass, at her hair, silken and beautiful, as it fell over her shoulders in luxurious ripples. She had read in stories, of girls who had sold their hair. She thought with a sigh that she might do it if hard pressed. This was the subject which possessed her mind, when a door opened below, and her landlady called up the stair:

"Miss Meers! Miss Meers! Will you come and speak to this lady?"

Nana arose quickly, and hurried to the little parlor on the first floor, where the lodgers usually received their visitors. As she entered, a lady who had been sitting on a chair by the window arose to greet her.

She was a frail little creature with great dark circles under her eyes. She wore a neatly-fitting dress of blue serge and a large sun hat, which looked as though it had been adjusted in a hurry without much thought as to the points of compass; her hands, which were ungloved, were white and slender, and her face fine and intellectual as it was, bore evidence of its owner's acquaintance with pain, mental or physical, or both. Nana had little chance to study it, for the young woman took a keen survey of her from head to foot, and said,

"You'll do."

Nana looked at her questioningly.

"I am Miss Sedling of the Palladian Art Academy," the stranger explained. "We are in trouble down there, and I have undertaken to settle matters. Our model went off in a huff this morning, and Mr. Hartman thought classes would have to be suspended until another could be secured. I happened to know Mrs. Yates, your landlady, who sometimes, you see, chances to have with her, persons glad of temporary employment, and I came to her for assistance in the dilemma. She has referred me to you. Will you come?"

An art academy! Nana found the prospect entrancing. She would gladly go.

"All you'll have to do is to wear a Roman costume and stand as you are placed," Miss Sedling went on to explain. "You will make a fine picture with a classic background. Our patron goddess must have directed my footsteps this morning."

Nana ran to get her hat. Her picture to be painted,

and in a Roman costume with a classic background !
How delightfully romantic !

She was soon ready, and as they walked along, her
companion waxed communicative.

" I like your looks," she said, " and it will give me
great pleasure to paint you. You will find posing
monotonous, I dare say, but they will pay you fifty
cents an hour. You did not ask me what they would
pay before you agreed to come. Why not ? "

" Oh, I was very glad to go! " exclaimed Nana.
" I have never seen an art school, and I consider it
very good fortune indeed to have my picture painted."

Miss Sedling smiled at her enthusiasm.

" Where have you lived all your life? " she asked.

" In the country."

"And you think the city is a wonderful place? "

" I—I was rather disappointed in it at first, but now
I am sure I shall like it," said Nana.

" Youth is very hopeful," Miss Sedling remarked,
with another odd smile upon her lips.

Nana wondered how old *she* was. She had a quick
elastic step, and her voice was light and young. But
there was such a worn expression upon her face.
Nana could not guess her age.

Miss Sedling cast another swift glance at Nana,
taking her in from head to foot.

" You are a little wild flower," she said at length.
" It is not often we have a model like you. I do not
intend any flattery. I speak as an artist. Never be
vain. Take the gifts which God has bestowed and
enjoy them humbly. I was once beautiful."

Nana glanced at the weary little face somewhat doubtfully, at which her companion smiled again.

" There is something more than mere physical beauty in the face which I admire. Do you know what that is?" Miss Sedling inquired.

Nana did not. Indeed, she was beginning to feel herself utterly insignificant beside this little woman, this real artist.

" I mean soul—expression. The face which tells a story."

" What story can mine tell?" Nana questioned wonderingly.

" It tells one."

" Do tell me what."

" You are interested in yourself, are you not? Well, it is but natural. Youth always is. It is not vanity. It is simplicity and—and curiosity. Youth is curious and it has a right to be. Youth stands on the brink of life and looks eagerly forward, proud and confident in its own little craft that soon must be launched upon the flood. Poor little boat! We may hope that it carries a good strong life line."

The two were silent for a moment. Then Miss Sedling spoke again.

"Are you visiting here?"

" No."

"Are your parents living?"

" No."

" Poor child! Did you come here expecting to work?"

" To work and study, if I can."

" To study what ? "

" Oh, I don't know. I am so ignorant. I want to know everything."

" You can not do that. However, mere knowledge is nothing. What one wants is development. You should study art."

" I should like to."

" Art is a refuge from the world and from yourself, that is, the study of it. I like you. I am city born, and you are something new and curious to me. I am used to hot-house roses and artificials. Sweet briars are rarities in the market. I am going to have you pose for me privately, later on. I want to paint you with a country background, and call you ' The Sweet Briar.' Do you like the idea ? "

" Oh, if you could only paint the little hills !" murmured Nana. " I should love to see them again."

" Are you homesick ? "

" No, only for the hills and the cattle, and — and —"

" You must tell me of them, and probably I shall be able to do it. We are nearing the Academy now, and I must give you a word of warning. You must not pay attention to anything you hear said. We can not afford to be sensitive in this world of work. No one who loves art for its own grand sake will annoy you, but there are some who may. However, always remember that I am your friend, and that I am about the oldest student in the place, which gives me a sort of distinction. I should advise you as soon as possible to change your mode of dressing. Yours is picturesque I allow, but rather old fashioned and countrified. Here we are."

The Academy grounds were spacious and green. In the center stood the building, which Nana thought very odd in shape, and Miss Sedling told her that it was built after an old Greek pattern. The halls were dark and even chilly. Miss Sedling led Nana upstairs into a small room with one grimy window, through the panes of which the sunlight struggled faintly. She then brought out from a cobwebby wardrobe, the Roman dress which was once white, perhaps, but of a decidedly negative tint now, and much the worse for wear. Nana was soon arrayed in its classic folds, and conducted in triumph before the class.

"She has captured one! She has captured one!" was the enthusiastic greeting. Nana thought it extremely rude. Her newly-found friend seemed to read her thoughts, and whispered:

"Never mind. This is the realm of art. Don't have any feelings. They are superfluous. You'll get used to it."

Nana was duly placed in pose, and after a few murmurs of admiration, the class fell to work.

Nana's task was no easy one. She was beginning to feel faint from standing so long, when some one remarked, in a mechanical tone:

"The model has moved her head."

"They talk as if I were a block of wood," thought Nana, but Miss Sedling was at her side, whispering

words of encouragement, and telling her that it was
time to rest.

" It isn't often Miss Thalia descends from her lofty
height," a student remarked loud enough to be heard,
as Nana passed into the cloak room, leaning on Miss
Sedling's arm.

"She is behaving strangely," was the answer.
" But really the model is pretty—more than pretty."

" That's nothing.   We've had pretty models before.
She's dowdy enough.   I saw them as they came into
the hall down stairs, before she put on the costume."

" There is no telling what Thalia will do.   She is
freakish.   She is an old student and a good one ; we
must respect, but thank goodness, we needn't imitate
her."

Nana took her place again when called, and so the
forenoon went by with alternate posing and resting.

" You'll be on time to-morrow?" a voice called
after her, as almost deaf and blind from over-exertion,
she turned to leave the wilderness of easels and canvas
for the last time that day.

" I will not fail," she replied, and hurried out.

Miss Sedling was in the dressing room to unpin the
ancient drapery, and help Nana to readjust her own
gown and hat.

" You are tired, are you not?" she said.   "To-
morrow I must see that you get to rest oftener.   But
you have captivated them all.   I heard Mr. Hartman
himself call you a sylph.   That ought to be enough to
rest you immediately, for Mr. Hartman seldom takes
time to be complimentary."

Nana's reflections were none too pleasant as she walked homeward. Notwithstanding the fact that Mr. Hartman had taken time to praise her, she vowed that nothing but the money would entice her into the Palladian Academy again. She had to live, and well it was for the unfinished picture. The remarks she had overheard concerning herself and her dress seemed more than she could bear ; but she would not be a laughing stock because of her old country made dress, which she had once thought so pretty. Sooner than that, she would sell her hair. With this idea, she repaired to the establishment of a well-known hair-dresser, immediately after dinner, which was very hurriedly eaten lest any delay should weaken her resolution.

She crept up the stairs and knocked timidly at the door. It was opened by a blustering young woman, with wiry hair, steel-gray eyes, and harsh, masculine voice.

" Well, miss, what can I do for you ? " she asked as Nana hesitated on the threshold.

" Do you buy hair here ? " the girl faltered.

" Yes, sometimes."

" Will—will you buy mine ? "

The woman stepped forward, and took one of Nana's curls between her fingers. She examined it critically for a moment, then said :

" Yes, I'll take it."

" What will you pay ? "

" Twenty-five cents an ounce."

" How many ounces are there ? "

" About six."

The vision of a new gown, ribbons, and gloves instantly vanished. It was a bitter disappointment. Nana slid into a chair and wept silently. The woman had produced a great pair of shears, and stood eyeing the sobbing girl half scornfully.

" Well, shall I take it ? Are you in need of bread ? "

Nana sprang to her feet, shot a swift glance at her questioner, then without a word of reply, left the place.

As she was returning to her lodging, a sign in the window of a dilapitated building caught her attention. It read : " Cash for Second Hand Books." Here was another hope. Nana had several books as good as new ; she would sell them.

A little old man in a shabby coat met her as she entered, and inquired with a smile, " What does the lady wish ? " However, when it was found that she had only come to see about disposing of a few volumes, his countenance fell, and he growled out :

" Got 'em with you ? "

" No, I came to see if you would take them."

" How can I tell ? I don't make bargains in no such way, Miss. You'll have to bring 'em if you want to sell 'em here."

" What do you pay ? "

" Oh, it depends. Can't tell until I see 'em."

Nana ran home to her room, and brought back her

books for the old man's inspection. He took them from her hand, turned them over, and shook his head. Nana's heart stood still.

'' Can't allow you more than fifty cents for the six.''

'' But see how new they are. I paid much more for them.''

'' Can't help that. I aint here for my health. I'll give you just what I said ; take it or leave it.''

'' Take them,'' said Nana when she saw that this was final.

The man counted out her money from a dirty little linen bag which he took from his pocket. Nana received it with a sigh and left the shop.

The result of this business transaction was a new collar and a tortoise shell hairpin such as the girls at the Academy wore. She bought them at a notion store on her way home. It was the best she could do, though it was but a step toward conventional fashion. The pin, she placed with pride in the fluffy pyramid of brown hair, which after several fruitless attempts, she succeeded in building up. It was entirely satisfactory as far as it went. She glanced repeatedly at her handiwork in the looking-glass, and thought what an utter transformation a trained gown would make in her appearance.

She had turned over a new leaf in life's text-book. The dreams of our ignorance turn to dust and ashes under the touch of Experience's hand. Nana resolved to follow the advise of Miss Sedling, to do away with all feeling, and expect nothing further at the hand of fate.

The next day found her at her place before the class
in the Palladian Academy, a little paler than usual,
but with a look of pride and determination about her
lips that no one could fail to notice. Miss Sedling
told her that Mr. Hartman intended to paint her por-
trait himself, he had found her so interesting, and
several of the older lady students were wild to have
her pose for them privately.

"I told them that I did not know whether you
would or not," Miss Sedling said.

"I—I need the money very much," said Nana ner-
vously.

"But it won't do to appear too anxious," warned
Miss Sedling. "Let me manage that. I'll have the
price of your sittings raised before you're a week
older."

CHAPTER IX.

THALIA.

NANA had been at the Academy three months
and was beginning to feel quite at home. Mr.
Hartman had induced a wealthy lady patron of the
school to take an interest in her, and she had begun
to study drawing with an under teacher, preparatory
to entering the life class.

She had realized her desire to possess a stylish
gown, and no one ever spoke of her now as dowdy.
She was considered a very fortunate young lady to
have been taken up by Mrs. Star, who kept a fine
house, went into society, and took a trip abroad whenever she pleased. Mrs. Star, it was rumored, had a
son also, and who could tell what might happen?
Miss Meers was beautiful enough to grace any position.

She was sitting in the lecture room one morning
almost concealed by the cast of Psyche, when she
heard her name mentioned.

" That girl," said a large woman in bright blue, to
an insignificant little creature with palette and brushes
under her arm, " that girl has a future before her."

" Has she any talent? "

" Hum, can't say. Divine gifts are nothing nowa-
days. She has a pretty face and insinuating manners.

I'll warrant Miss Sedling wishes she'd left her in her wretched boarding house to starve.''

''How so?''

''Because she has what Miss Sedling should have.''

''What's that?''

''Mr. Hartman's favor and Mrs. Star's support.''

''Miss Sedling is always admiring her.''

''Yes, but that's a blind. How can she do otherwise? Do you suppose she's going to rejoice in Mr. Hartman's infatuation, when you know she's dead in love with him herself?''

''He seems to be rather prejudiced in her favor too. Do you think they'll ever marry?''

''Marry! Land sakes, no! Thalia is half dead with consumption. The model—I mean Miss Meers, has the upper hand.''

The woman in blue was one whom Nana had often seen pacing up and down the corridor, conversing earnestly with a group of eager listeners, while others passed by with an odd smile remarking half audibly, ''The talking machine.''

Nana felt hurt at what she had heard. She had not seen Miss Sedling for some time. Was what the woman said really true? Had she lost the kind regard of the friend she loved so much?

The two gossips sat down and began to sketch the very Psyche behind which the girl sat, keeping up their chatter meanwhile. Presently the door opened, and the subject was immediately changed. The woman in blue burst out with:

"What life is more happy than that of the student, especially the student of an art? While others walk the earth, he treads the clouds. He may not succeed in the world's sense of the word, but after all, is he a failure? Some poet has said that even our failures are a prophecy. If this life is all, then what are our longings created for? Are those who yearn for the unattainable, simply questions without answers?"

The girl who had just come in joined the group and said:

"I see, Mrs. France, that you are trying to vindicate my right to existence. Bravo! And thrice again, bravo! You are supremely charitable to concede me the privilege. Few there are who care how much a poor glow-worm may struggle to let its little light shine for eyes that see, smile, and forget, but the worm understands and if it can enjoy its brief hour of diminutive triumph, let it, for there are worms and worms, and to-morrow it dies and is never missed."

"Who calls you a failure, Miss Sedling?"

"No one has dared as yet. But the glow-worm knows that she is not the moon."

"You are the brightest star among us, Miss Sedling."

"I am a meteor," the girl rejoined.

"If you were Miss Meers, you would not speak in that way. I don't doubt that she thinks herself a genius."

"Miss Meers has health and spirit and beauty. She will succeed easier than others. I should call life worth the living if I were like her."

The others exchanged meaning glances.

"Always raving over superficiality," remarked Mrs. France.

"Well, what is the use of always keeping our best admiration for abstractions? I adore realities. I have always regarded soul as the fountain head of expression, but I have never seen a soul. The outer mask is all I have before which to bow."

"But there is that subtle something which distinguishes the work of genius from that of the ordinary mortal. Have you no feelings of exaltation in the presence of that?"

"I consider that subtle something to be the result of patient, long-suffering labor, experience and observation."

"Gross materialist! I am surprised that a woman of your talent should set so little store by it."

"Well, I'd rather by far possess all the gowns in Madame Rambeau's window at present, than half the stuff, essence, or whatever you call my talent. I always walk that way in order to look at those gowns, which I am ready to fall down on my face before. They transform the bisque figures on which they are draped into goddesses. It is the externals that make life worth living."

"How about this Miss Meers, anyway?"

"Miss Meers? Oh, its been an age since I've seen the child. She doesn't need me now."

"What does she study?"

"Drawing principally. She is getting ready for the

life class, I understand. She attends the lectures too, I think, for the Theory. I despise theories. I flee from them as from a pestilence. My forte is practice. I don't want books or talks or sputterings which they dignify by the name of criticism. What I want is life, life pure and simple, life with all its beauty and all its ugliness."

"You mean for your art work."

"Certainly. Isn't art my life?"

"You contradict yourself. A little while ago you said you would forego success for a new gown."

"Did I say that? Were those my exact words? Well, let it pass, at any rate. We all contradict our-selves. When a certain passion sways us, we are one being, and when that passes away, we are another."

"Has she any talent—Miss Meers, I mean? What does she intend to make of herself?"

"I don't know. Her plans are probably not yet well defined. She has simply caught the art fever because it is in the atmosphere. But she will succeed. She was made for success."

"Is Mr. Hartman fond of her?"

"I believe he considers her a very promising student. However, I have not heard him speak of her often."

Miss Meers scanned the features of the pale girl, from worn young brow to delicately pointed chin. They were as symmetrical as a marble masterpiece, but they were not beautiful; they were too wan for that. Nana felt that if she had put an obstacle in the way of Miss

Sedling's happiness, she could never forgive herself.

With a few more comments, the woman in blue and her companion, gathering up their drawing materials, took their leave, as the clock had struck ten, and they were due at private appointments with an instructor. When they had disappeared through the door, Nana emerged from her hiding place.

"I have heard it all!" she cried, throwing her arms about her friend, and bursting into tears.

"Tush! Tush! Don't be volcanic. It doesn't pay," Miss Sedling replied, stroking her hair.

"But they said—they said before you came in, that I was standing in your light, that I was making you miserable."

"And you kept hid and listened?"

"Yes."

"That was not etiquette, but it was perfectly proper in the unconventional sense, that is, if you wanted to run the risk of making yourself miserable. I speak to you as to a sensitive plant. When a few more summer suns have showered their scorching light upon you, I can advise differently. But truly, nothing that anybody says is worth the trouble of contradicting."

"But if none of it is true, why did you keep yourself from me? I do need you as much as I ever did. I have been very lonely."

"Mrs. Star is your patroness now, and not Thalia Sedling. Mrs. Star is very exclusive and particular. Does she visit you much?"

"Very seldom."

"And when she does?"

"She is polite and kind."

"Does she give you much advice?"

"Yes, about studying hard."

"Has she said anything about your associates?"

"No."

"Well, you see, I was once an actress. There is a prejudice against the calling, you know, especially among persons of Mrs. Star's class. An art school is supposed to be a democracy, and perhaps it is, but I was afraid that your friend, the great lady, might object to me, and I did not want to stand in your light. You have your way to make in the world. Mine is already made."

Nana looked at her companion admiringly.

"And you were really an actress," she said.

"Yes," answered Miss Sedling with a smile.

"Oh, how I envy you! How I should like to be an actress! I think it is the greatest profession in the world."

"So do I, if there is any profession that is really great. Somehow, I think that the farmer at work in his field has more time for sentiment and romance than we who are supposed to dwell in the midst of it. If the farmer only knew how!"

"Some do," said Nana thinking with a pang of Lucky Fielding whom she had set out with all her heart to forget, even if she must force herself to fall in love with some one else in order to do it.

"But why did you ever leave the stage?" she inquired after a moment of silence. "Did you like painting better?"

"I have not really left it, though I do not do the work I once did. My health will not permit. I used to play leading comic parts. That is the reason why they call me Thalia. Quite often in the evening, I go as supernumerary when any is needed, to help eke out my income, as my pictures won't sell. It is the life I love. I love the theatre, even its dust and tawdry decorations which newspaper people declare so disenchanting. I love the hustle and bustle behind the scenes. I love to hear the soubrettes quarrel over curling irons and looking glasses, and to peep through a hole in some side curtain to see the audience sobbing or convulsed with laughter. Whenever I come across the name of an old fellow worker of days gone by, cut or scrawled on the walls of a dressing room, I kiss it as fervently as a heathen does his idol."

"How odd! I have heard it said that you had a history."

"So I have. A lady once asked me if I had not, and I told her yes, two of them, a History of the World, and one of the United States. You must come to my room some time and I will show you my box of wigs and masks."

"How very, very strange!"

"Not at all. Things may seem so, viewed at a distance, but when you have once crossed the border and entered the kingdom, all is natural and even commonplace."

"They said that—that—"

"What did they say? Come, confess — don't hesitate."

"That you were Mr. Hartman's favorite student before I came, and that—"

"That I was in love with him. Go on."

"How did you know?"

"How do we know anything? I have five very acute senses. Go on."

"They said that Mrs. Star was doing for me what she ought to do for you."

"Nonsense. They don't know what they are talking of. Did you know that Mr. Hartman is engaged to Mrs. Star?"

"Is it possible?"

"Everything is possible. Some of the strange things of life would look so strange in a book that people would declare it to be extravaganza. Not that there is anything so very strange about this match, however. Mrs. Star, I suppose, is as desirable as any woman, and we must own that Mr. Hartman is a man to know and worship. At least, the ideal Mr. Hartman is — we may not know the real. But I must bid you good-bye, now, for there goes the half-past ten bell. Can I see you this evening? No, I have a novel appointment to fill at six, and after that I shall be too tired. But say, would you care to join me in my walk at six sharp?"

"Where do you go—to the theatre?"

"No. A little newsboy just starting into business,

is very ill and afraid he'll lose his few customers.   He
has only about twenty, but they mean bread to himself and little brother.   I have agreed to carry his
papers for him, they are so few, and the customers are
quite near together.   I know it is not a ladylike thing
to do.   The ladylike thing would be to shed a few
tears, and wish it were not so, or give the little suf-
ferer a few pennies, then go off, and forget him.   It's
a fine lark, bless you.   I've done it two nights in suc-
cession.   Will you come, and treat yourself to a new
experience?"

"Yes.   At six, you say?"

"At six on the corner of Fifth and K street.   That's
near the news office where Barney trades.   Then,
we'll have supper at the Alhambra like two veritable
Bohemians.   Will Mrs. Star object to your going?"

" I don't think she'll care.   I think she would consider that you were doing a very noble thing.   I am
proud of you."

The evening was damp and foggy, but Thalia was
at the trysting place, walking up and down impatiently, when Nana came in sight.   She coughed
slightly when she opened her mouth to reply to
Nana's greeting, and the latter inquired concernedly:

"Ought you to be out, to-night, dear?"

" I never fail when I have promised anything.   Besides, making that little Irish boy happy is worth a
year or two of life.   You should see his big, feverish
eyes shine when I put the pennies into his hand.   He
would fight all L for my sake, Barney would.   But

here is the news office. Notice the puzzled look in
the clerk's eyes when I ask him for the papers. I
don't explain anything. I like to keep him wondering."

The papers were duly handed to their rightful
recipients, and the supper at the Alhambra was eaten
with keen zest. As they stepped into the street again,
a thought struck Nana.

" They say that Mrs. Star has a son," she said.

" Yes," returned Thalia, " but he's feeble minded.
I suppose they have been romancing about him.
Were they planning to marry him to either of us ? "

"I have heard so."

Thalia laughed, and slipping her hand through
Nana's arm, said:

" We'd better step up. I am afraid it's going to
rain."

The storm overtook them, however, despite their
attempt to hasten home, and resulted in Thalia's
retiring with a severe cold. On the following day
Nana was in the cloak room putting on her wrap and
hat to pay the invalid a visit, and receiving messages
of condolence to carry in the name of various acquaintances, when in walked the object of their com-
miseration, looking radiant.

"Great news!" she shouted, waving her hand
above her head. "My picture has gone to the exhibition and will have a good place. I am almost
sure of honorable mention. Some have hinted that I
may take the European prize. Who'll wager me
that I don't ? "

"I heard that you were very ill last night. How is it you are here to-day?" inquired Mrs. France.

The girl sat down upon the floor, and lifted her eyes to her questioner's face.

"Last night was last night, and to-day is to-day."

"But ought you to be out? Ought you not to wait until you feel better?"

"If I did that, what should I ever accomplish? It would be a longer wait than I dare make, my dear."

"Are you better?" said Nana when the lesson bell rang, and the two were left alone in the cloak room.

"I don't know. I am told not. The doctor says I must be careful. I trust I shall be. I shall not go to the theatre for three weeks at least. Will that not be a sacrifice?"

"Three weeks is not a long time."

"Is it not? Why, my child, how long are your eternities? But come to my room. It is not your lesson hour, and I want you to see my den and its contents by daylight. Besides, there is the picture I talked of beginning so long ago, 'The Sweet Briar,' I mean. I wish I'd done that for the exhibition. I must arrange with you to begin it immediately."

It was a rare honor to be invited to Thalia's studio. Nana gazed about the poor, half-furnished apartment with the same wonder with which she surveyed everything that pertained to Miss Sedling. There were the customary easels and pictures, palettes and brushes; but the paintings on the easels were no more ordinary than was the creator of them. Nana noted two in particular. One, "Waiting for the Cue," represented a young girl, dressed in pure white, standing in the wing of a theatre, finger on lip, a look of pleased expectation mingled with faint anxiety in her eyes, and one foot advanced ready to spring forward when the signal should come. The other was called "The Drop Curtain." It was evidently a companion piece, for the features of the second woman bore a strong resemblance to those of the first. She lay upon an iron bed in a wretched room, her eyes half closed, and a look of death upon her white, drawn face.

There were books, poems, dramas and novels lying everywhere in the studio. A decrepit table stood in one corner, on which was an unfinished manuscript play, a tattered copy of "The Hunchback," scarred by annotations and cutting, and a bust of Moliere.

"I keep those," said Thalia in the midst of a fit of coughing, "'To hold together what I was and am,' as Mrs. Browning puts it. I don't want to get my several separate identities mixed, or to forget that I am I, if you can understand that better. That is my kitchen and dining-room behind yon curtain. I have an enchanting little coffee-pot, and will show you by and by how well the Muse can brew the popular beverage, if I don't forget. Has Mrs. Star scolded you for your last night's folly?"

"No. I have not seen her. Besides, how should she know?"

"Gossip is like thistle-down; it flies. Mrs. Star is very well known and I'll wager you that more people know you, and know that you are the young lady she's educating than you imagine."

"How do you happen to know so much of her? Are you personally acquainted?"

"I am a sort of step-niece, that is all. I am the adopted daughter of the lady who married her brother. Both are dead now."

The atmosphere of the room was chilly, and Nana was obliged to shiver now and then. She thought how bad it was for Thalia's cough. She looked at her friend's blue serge, which though still neat, was becoming old and threadbare about the elbows. It made her heart ache to see it. Here was the girl whom everybody called a genius, whose life everybody thought so romantic, sitting before her, pale and worn from the struggle for existence. It moved her to inquire,

"Do you think Mrs. Star would have done anything for you if I had not come?"

"No. I am not pretty like you."

"But you are attractive—yes, and you are beautiful."

"In the artistic sense, perhaps—sometimes. But you are beautiful in every sense at all times. Don't worry your little head any more. I dare say Mrs. Star would patronize me now in a gingerly way to please Mr. Hartman, if I would allow it. Indeed he has intimated as much to me. But I have depended upon myself so long that I can not bear the idea of reflected glory. Ishmael loveth the desert. Mr

Hartman thinks me obstinate and Mrs. Star does not insist. The son calls it a 'deuced shame,' but his words carry little weight."

"How old is the son? Is he really so sadly afflicted?"

"He is some twenty four, handsome enough, but in reality weak. Oh dear, let's change the subject! I wish you'd call me Louise, hereafter. That is my own old name. It has been a long time since I've heard it. It seems to me you'd make music of it with that exquisite voice of yours. Some one else used to say it just as you would, I fancy, but that's all gone by now. Look what has taken its place!" and the girl dragged from beneath her bed a box of wigs and masks, hideous, Nana thought most of them.

"They have kept my heart from breaking many a time, the darlings!" cried Thalia, then broke down and coughed again.

"You think this is dreadful," she resumed when the paroxysm had passed, laughing in Nana's anxious face. "But I am used to it. It has been several years since I've seen a well day. Through it all art has been my consolation, divine, all compensating art. They have said for some time that I am likely to die but I laugh at them. *I* die! ha, ha!"

The girl threw her head back against the old plush cushion of the chair in which she sat, and gave vent to a long, low peal of mirthless laughter.

Presently her expression changed to one of intense agony.

"I can not die!" she cried starting forward, and burying her nails in either temple. "I will not die! I have too much to do! I love this body, weak and faulty as it is. I don't want to lose my identity and become all soul. I want to be myself, myself! I don't want to dwell in the midst of peace and perfection,— I should stagnate utterly. Give me humanity, foolish, perverse, wicked humanity! Give me the world full of unwritten tragedy and comedy! I'd forego heaven for that!"

After this outburst she lay back against her cushion for a moment quite exhausted, then rousing herself, began to talk lightly of ordinary things, prepared coffee and tea-cakes for her visitor and behaved as if nothing had happened.

The exhibition day came. Thalia received her honorable mention with prophecies of the European prize at no late day in her career. Nana found her sitting against a mass of framework in the gallery, her eyes closed and looking very tired.

"Are you not pleased with your success?" Nana inquired, taking her hand.

"What is success?" murmured the pale girl, half to herself. "Success—only a clapping of hands, a word or two of congratulation,and you are forgotten."

The next instant, she looked up and smiled.

"Come to my room to-morrow," she said. "I must finish 'The Sweet Briar.' I wish I had finished it before the exhibition. It might have sold."

"Are you well enough to paint?"

"To paint you—yes. It is not toil but pleasure. I must finish 'The Sweet Briar'—then let the skies fall."

But the picture was never finished. When the next day arrived, Miss Sedling found herself too tired to do good work, and dismissed her model at the end of an hour. She did not explain that for two days she had been living on strong tea and hope—hope that her prize picture "Evening at Bethlehem," would sell. When night came, she dragged herself out of bed where she had spent the afternoon, and contrary to her resolution not to do so until the end of three weeks, she went to the theatre to earn the dollar which would sustain her for several days longer. The exertion, together with an added cold, was more than her weakened frame could endure. It brought on a relapse, and the young artist was so ill that the care which could be given her in her room was deemed insufficient, and she was removed to a public ward of the city hospital.

Here several days later, the curtain fell on Thalia Sedling's life.

There was a great sensation at the Academy. Students gathered about in the halls, talking in whispers. The class rooms were draped in black, and Mrs. Star very kindly brought flowers for the funeral. A reporter interviewed Mr. Hartman, and soon after, the story got abroad, and there began to be a great demand for the pictures painted by the girl who had lived and died so romantically. Alas that romance should be so hard to live !

At the grave, Bernard Star stood beside Nana. Her beauty was softened into almost saint-like loveliness by the solemnity of the hour. When the services were at an end, he turned to her and said:

"You are Miss Sedling's friend, are you not—the original of 'The Sweet Briar'? I should know you anywhere."

"I am Miss Meers," the girl returned.

"It is a shame," he went on, walking beside her as she started to leave the cemetery "I always told mother so. I admired Miss Sedling very much. Will you be my friend for her sake?"

Nana held out her hand, which was warmly pressed by the son of Mrs. Star.

CHAPTER X.

AT THE ROYSTER FARM. LUND COMES INTO HIS INHERITANCE.

"ANY news?" inquired Mrs. Royster of Lund, as he came in with heavy, dragging step, and threw himself into a chair. Her voice was more metallic than ever, her eyes more sunken, and her face more sallow, the result of anxious days and sleepless nights.

She had never loved Nana; but the girl was gone, and the weight was upon her conscience. In committing an error, we never dream how poignant will be the repentance which is sure to follow the failure of our plans.

Lund had no news.

"Well, I'm sure it ain't my fault," she whined, rocking to and fro; then unable to bear the gnawing weight upon her soul, she burst out with:

"Do you think it is my fault?"

Lund shook his head dismally. It was an equivocal gesture. She felt that it did not absolve her. She had never had any respect for Lund, and she had none now, but the heart in distress cries out to the nearest living creature at hand, even though that creature be a dog. The brain tired out with fighting its own battles, seeks elsewhere for an ally to buoy up its courage a day, an hour, a minute longer; recklessly, hopelessly often, as a drowning man clutches at a straw.

Bub Royster came home a little later. He too had been searching for the missing girl, but had waited for a chance to ride from the Bend with a neighbor, whereas Lund had come on foot. Bub hated Nana, and but for the urging of his mother and Rose Dolby, would have been heartily glad to let her go. Joe Slocum dropped in about the same time to inquire as to the success of the search. He was a shrewd man and his advice was of much service. As far as his knowledge extended, Joe Slocum was not bad. He could see no reason why Nana should have anything against him. He had always been good to her, and had intended to make her a kind husband; but since she had taken such means to rid herself of him, he wished he had let her have her own way. Aside from his admiration for Nana, he had regarded the affair as a very legitimate business transaction, but there was still man enough in him to recognize that she had some right to think in the matter, now that she had taken it in defiance of circumstances.

Of Lund's loss and sorrow, we need not speak. It was unvarnished and sincere.

Rumor had spread about the settlement that Lucky Fielding had gone to the Upper Missouri, to get himself a wife. Nevertheless, he returned from his trip without one, determined to confess the object of his deception to Nana, who by this time should have had ample opportunity to miss him, and mend her manners. He was accustomed to easy victories in all matters, and expected the same thing here. His arrogance soon received a telling blow. Nana had never spoken to him of her one-sided engagement to Joe Slocum. Since her entrance into young woman-hood, it had become but a dim memory to her. Lucky listened in utter amazement to his sister's account of Nana's trouble and her wildly courageous act; then notwithstanding all former quarrels, he repaired to the Royster's to inquire more fully into the affair, and join them in their endeavor to recover the missing one.

Lund saw him coming, and met him at the door. They shook hands, and Lucky was conducted forth-with into the midst of the family council. He was joyfully received by Mrs. Royster, but Bub's greeting was sullen and morose. Lucky did not care. He sat down among them to talk the matter over.

"It beats me how the kid could have kept out o' sight so long," mused Joe Slocum sadly. "She hadn't no acquaintances in the city, had she?"

"No," answered Bub.

"Maybe she's dead," suggested Mrs. Royster with a wail.

Bub cried down this idea. Nana was a girl who could look out for herself. Joe Slocum seconded this confident affirmation.

"It is a sad case, a sad case," went on Slocum in tones of apology to Lucky, "but I can't see what we're to do. We've tried everything."

"Except the ounce of prevention," Lucky was about to say, but checked himself as he recollected that he too was not blameless in the affair.

"Let's advertise again," suggested Lund.

"'Twon't do any good," said Bub. "And advertisin' costs money."

"Never mind the money!" shrieked Mrs. Royster hysterically. "If money will find her, use it. Take everything I've got! The Lord knows it wa'n't my doin's. I did as well by the girl as I could—I did as well as I knew how."

All looked at her.

"Be quiet, mother," said Bub.

"Who said you was to blame?" Slocum inquired.

"I can tell by the way he looks at me that he thinks so!" she cried indicating Lucky with one bony finger. "I can tell by the way they look at me," with a scared glance in the direction of Slocum and Lund.

"Mother," said Bub savagely, "do hush."

"He told me on his dyin' bed," she continued; "he told me, but I didn't heed—but I swear I hain't been all to blame—I hain't been all to blame!"

All eyes were riveted upon her face, the features of which were set and white as those of the dead. Presently she sank on her knees trembling and moaning:

"O God, strike me dead—strike me dead this minute—I deserve it, but I hain't been all to blame!"

Consternation reigned. Joe was first to act. He brought a cup of water which he dashed into her face, then called the girls, and Mrs. Royster was carried away still raving, and protesting her innocence.

"Never let the women into anything," Bub growled. "They always make a fuss. We're in a bad enough mess already without having it made worse."

"She shows some heart though," said Slocum, "and that's more'n I ever give her credit fur."

A renewed search for Nana was immediately begun. They advertised in the papers again, and set the police to work; but these men seemed to look everywhere but in the right place, and Nana Meers continued to follow her life in the beautiful suburbs of L, striving to forget that she had ever been anything else than pretty Miss Meers, student of the Palladian Academy of Art. What omniscient policeman would have thought of looking for such a girl there? Nana was changed too, for she no longer wore her hair in curls, and her brown cotton delaine dress and sailor hat had long since been consigned to the flames. They would never have known her, at any rate; and by some freak of the goddess who presides over our destinies, neither she nor any of her acquaintances had come across the notice in the L dailies, inquiring for information concerning her.

*   *   *   *   *   *

It was midwinter. Bub Royster had gone to town for the mail, and Lucky Fielding, having returned from a long and fruitless search for Nana, had called at the Roysters' to talk with Lund, not because he had any respect for the fellow, but because Lund was the only one who seemed to regard him as the girl's best friend.   It pleased Lucky to be so regarded, no matter from what source.

As they sat together to-day, Lund made a startling confession.

" I loved her," he said with a growing light on his long, gaunt features.   " I loved her as well, likely, as you.   I didn't know how to show it, but I did the best I could.   It didn't do any good, and it never would.   She loved you.   You're bright and hand-some, and her style.   She'd never think of marrying a fellow like me."

Lucky was touched by these words.   He felt that he ought to reply, but did not know what to say;   so of course he blundered.

" She might have, Lund.   You don't know."

" You're a tryin' to fool me," Lund returned. " You're a tryin' to be kind, and I'm much obliged to you.   But I know.   I love the little 'un, and many's the time I've thought of her, and prayed to God with tears in my eyes.   I didn't pray for what I knew couldn't happen, but I wished the angels might have a kindly eye to her while she was there without friends and without a home.   And I wished that by and by she might be found and brought back to be your wife, Lucky, for I know she'd be happy so."

Lucky never prayed.   He had faith in his own strong will, his indomitable perseverance, but not in prayer.   The passing years had almost obliterated the religious beliefs of his boyhood. He no longer had trust in a guiding providence, but looked upon man as a creature born into the world to take his chances whatever they might be. He did not deny the existence of a supreme being, nor of a life hereafter; but he expected no reward until that life should come, when souls stripped of the fleshy mold that holds them imprisoned, should stand free of all environment that tends to stunt or distort, to grow into shapes divine like unto their creator. In this, Lucky was inconsistent as we all are. The belief, which he called sensible and liberal, but which is yet open to attack as being visionary, did not teach him charity for the Roysters, or else he was willing to reserve his admiration for them until the time should come when they should deserve it. The fact is, he did not spend much of his life looking beyond his daily duties. They surrounded him, he could see them, they were realities. Many a time of late he had been discouraged, and even now, he felt that he was hoping against hope. He had no more respect for Lund than he ever had, but somehow as he surveyed the great awkward fellow sitting there in the hazy light of the winter afternoon, his haggard face bowed upon his hands, and his lank form quaking with emotion, Lucky's heart softened and a mist gathered before his eyes. He held out his hand.

"Old man," he said with more warmth in his voice than was his wont when addressing Lund, "you're a trump. To-morrow we'll start out to search for her again, and we'll start together."

All day it had threatened storm. Bub Royster had not yet returned. His mother was filled with anxiety lest it should overtake him on his way. Lund and Lucky still sat by the fire, talking of Nana when a mingled rush and roar fell upon their ears, the meaning of which they knew, and in another instant the room was so dark that they could scarcely see each other.

" I wonder if he can be out in this ? " said Lund, as he rose to light a lamp.

Lucky did not reply. It was no affair of his. Bub Royster was at liberty to take care of himself, as far as Lucky was concerned.

There were a few fierce puffs of wind that shook the house and caused the shutters to rattle with a dreary sound. Then the storm bore down steadily, carrying the snow, which had lain for days on the ground, before it. Rain began to fall, and to freeze as it fell. Lund shivered as he listened to its beating against the pane.

Presently Mrs. Royster entered with her apron over her face.

" Oh, my boy, my boy ! " she wailed. " You that I've toiled and suffered for—you that I've lied and sinned for—to think you've got to die like this ! " She broke into a fit of hysterical sobbing.

Lund turned to Lucky. " Pore thing ! " he said sympathetically.

" You pity her, do you ? " was Lucky's incredulous retort.

"Yes, I do," returned Lund, "and I'm goin' out to see if he's on the road. It'll ease her mind, for I can find my way around the country better than most people, I've been about so much and know it so well. Besides, he's apt not to be quite himself after he's been to town. 'Tain't always so, but sometimes."

"You're a fool, Lund," said Lucky. "Think how bad he's treated you."

"Yes, I know it," returned Lund, "I know it. I've been kicked and cussed and starved by him, and I know it would serve him right, but I can't let him die out there like a dog, with his mother's cryin' in my ears."

Lund got his ragged overcoat and put it on; turning to Lucky, he said:

"Maybe I shan't come back alive, and if I don't, tell her I loved her better'n my own life, and would have died to save her trouble." After which, opening the door, he plunged out into the storm, muttering to himself: "It would serve him right, for the way he's treated her and the way he's treated me; but I can't let him die out there like a dog."

On he stumbled, through snow-drifts knee-deep, striking now and then a hidden wagon rut that tripped and almost threw him, struggling against a fierce wind that nearly took away his breath, with nothing but instinct to guide him in his choice of route. In all his twenty years of life on the prairie, Lund had never seen so mad a storm, yet he had no thought of turning back.

He had traveled about two miles, when the wind, blowing directly in his face, brought to him a sound which was something like a groan. He quickened his pace, shouting aloud as he did so, but the wind carried his voice in an opposite direction.

Then his feet struck against some object in his path; stooping over, he felt with numb fingers the garments of a man.

"Bub, Bub Royster!" he shouted, shaking the prostrate form with all the strength he possessed, "Here, rouse up! your mother's a cryin' her heart out for you at home. Come, rouse up!"

After much effort on the part of Lund, Bub, for it was he, regained interest enough in life to struggle to his feet, muttering drowsily meanwhile.

"Pity you can't let a fellow alone."

"Do you know where you be?" urged Lund. "Come, wake up, and step forward; lively now! Think about your mother and Rose Dolby—think of Rose!"

Thus he dragged his bitterest enemy along, out of the very jaws of death. The wind had shifted about, and blew directly in his face again. His task was no easy one. Bub hung like a dead weight upon him, he felt his body becoming weary with its prolonged effort, and the storm was rapidly increasing in fury.

It seemed that they had traveled for hours, when Bub, who had been slowly recovering from his fit of stupidity, said in hopeless tones:

"It's no use. We're lost. We might as well give up."

Lund had for a long time been oppressed with the same fear. He stood still for a moment to collect his thoughts, and, peering forward in the blinding snow, caught the red gleam of a light.

" Look ! there's a house !" he cried joyfully, "and it ain't more'n thirty rods away, I'll be bound ! Don't you see the red fire through the window ? "

The house from which the firelight came happened to be farmer Dolby's. It was Rose who welcomed them at the door. She was appalled when she came to know how near her lover had been to death, and overjoyed at his rescue. More fuel was thrown upon the fire, which blazed up invitingly. Bub was immediately wrapped in soft blankets, and lay sipping hot drinks prepared for him by loving hands.

Lund looked yearningly at the fire, but did not sit down. The Dolbys pressed him to stay, but he shook his head.

" Take care o' him. He needs it worse than me," he said. " I must get home and tell his mother. She's nigh gone crazy a worryin' over him." So saying, he lifted the latch, and in spite of their protests, started for home.

" Do you suppose anything will happen to him ?" asked Rose breathlessly when he had disappeared from sight in the thick of the flying snow.

" Never fear," answered Bub carelessly. " He knows the prairie like a horse does. He'll get home all right."

Rose brightened at this hopeful assurance, and in

the joy of her lover's society soon forgot Lund.

Meanwhile Lund was plodding along in the snow. The storm showed no signs of abating. The wind shifted rapidly from one direction to another, and the drifts piled themselves higher and higher in his path.

He did not realize that he was cold. Indeed, he felt very warm now. A little fringe of icicles, caused by his congealing breath, gathered round the edge of his hat and on his eyelashes, but he did not trouble himself to brush them away.

As he tramped on, he felt his limbs grow heavy, and a sensation of drowsiness crept over him. The feeling grew, until he became quite dazed. Finally his feet seemed stationery, and he felt himself gradually sinking into the drifts. He struggled feebly for a moment to extricate himself, then lay down, thinking to rest and get breath before resuming his journey.

The snow drifted over him, and he went to sleep.

CHAPTER XI.

MRS. STAR–HARTMAN.

MR. HARTMAN was becoming dreamy and abstracted. As the girls of the Academy put it, he walked with his head in the clouds. Ever and again, a tender smile played round his lips, that was not for anything he saw or heard. Now and then he was absent from the class room, and Miss Thatcher substituted in his place. It was whispered among the students that he was rehearsing for his wedding, which was to take place in the Protestant Episcopal Church very soon.

Nana listened while the others chattered of the preparations, the account of which they had read in the society papers, where even the mysteries of the designated rehearsals were dragged forth to pander to the public appetite. Nana heard with an indescribable sensation of spiritual nausea. Innocent, and full of that romance known chiefly to youth, that sentiment which if not divine, borders closely upon divinity, she felt the artificiality of the proceeding to the core. It was too much like preparing for a show, she thought. It seemed unworthy of a man like Mr. Hartman. Marriage to her was a sacred ordinance, and anything else than spontaneity and simplicity attending its details was a profanation.

But when the wedding day arrived, the excitement
of the hour possessed her, and she almost forgot her
former feelings. She received her invitation to be
present at the ceremony along with the other students.
She had expected as a *protégée* of Mrs. Star, an
invitation to the grand ball to be given at the residence
of the bride in the evening, but none came. She
wondered at this; she was fond of dancing, and could
dance as well as the best. Bernard Star was an
enthusiastic admirer of hers and a warm friend. Why
had she received no card?

Truly, Bernard Star had been a friend. He had
sent her costly bouquets every week, and had called
even oftener than Nana liked. He was a handsome
fellow worthy the brush of a painter. The girls at the
Academy had nick-named him "The Adonis in
Broadcloth." Yes, he was very fine to look at, and
with many persons his physical beauty was enough to
atone for his quite perceptible weakness of character.
Wealth too, covers such a multitude of sins. Bernard
Star was considered everywhere a "good catch."

Nana was not worldly; it was not that Bernard Star
was rich that she gave him a thought. She was
endeavoring to crush out her old love, and her heart
reached forth to the shadow of a new infatuation as a
welcome anodyne. She was young, and if she accepted the attentions of Mrs. Star's son in this spirit,
who can blame her?

Nana had never been asked to the house of Mrs.
Star except for private interviews with that lady.

Mrs. Star was even ignorant of her son's regard for the girl. He knew his mother and was afraid of her and Nana's name had never passed between them. Mrs. Star had undertaken Nana's education because Mr. Hartman had requested her to do so; she had undertaken a financial, not a social responsibility and she had no notion of undertaking the latter. She was a social queen and wanted no rival in her little world. If she were jealous of Nana's place in Mr. Hartman's regard it was not policy to show it.

The wedding was gotten through very satisfactorily. The bride was lovely enough to suit the most fastidious critic, and the bridegroom was proud and nervous as bridegrooms are wont to be. Nana sat in her seat with tense muscles, watching him sympathetically as the ceremony proceeded. When at last it was safely over, and Mr. and Mrs. Hartman had entered their carriage, she breathed a sigh of relief.

She had hoped up to the time the grand ball began that she had been overlooked, and that an invitation and apology for the delay would yet come. She was disappointed. In the evening, several of the Academy girls proposed a stroll past the house where the festivities were going on, as sidewalk room could not be prohibited them, and they purposed using all the privileges they possessed.

Nana scorned the idea as indelicate and common, but finally her curiosity got the better of her sense of propriety, and she consented to go.

The party outside was not a whit less merry than

the one indoors. They promenaded by twos up and down in the cool air, fanning themselves with boughs picked from the bride's own ornamental trees. They criticised to their fill each coming guest, enjoyed the lights in the windows and on the lawn, drank in the music as it floated across the garden, and let their hearts swell with the measures, just as if they had a right. The abandon was delicious; even Nana forgot herself in the intoxication of it, and laughed and talked as loudly as the others. Still she reproached herself as she laid her head upon her pillow that night. It was an extremely rude and improper thing to do. Mr. and Mrs. Hartman were her friends. They had simply overlooked her in sending invitations, and she had behaved in a very ungrateful manner towards them.

A week or so after, at the breakfast table, Bernard Star, more at his ease than usual with his mother because of the presence of Mr. Hartman, remarked in his lazy, drawling fashion:

" Why was not the beautiful Miss Meers at the ball? You surely invited her, mother? "

" Indeed I did not ! " was the rather sharp reply.

"Ah," the son continued, " that accounts for it; I wondered why she was with those girls who were looking on from the street. I took it as almost an insult, by Jove, but now I don't wonder."

" How do you know she was there? "

"I heard her laugh. I would know it among a thousand."

"Hum! I was not aware that you had the pleasure of the young lady's acquaintance. Where did you meet her, pray?" with a sarcastic smile.

"Almost anywhere but in my mother's drawing-room. Why do you treat her so, mother? Are you not her friend? Don't you admire her?"

"No, I do not and I trust that you, Bernard, will use the little common sense you have, and not go to falling in love with her in earnest. If you have merely carried on a flirtation with her somewhere and somehow, all well and good; I hold flirting to be an innocent amusement. However, you must make up your mind to break it off at once, as I consider her a dangerous person to tamper with, inasmuch as she is apparently so fascinating and you so easily led. You must make a match that will not shame your family."

Mr. Hartman looked up quickly. He was beginning to discover a new phase in the character of his charming wife.

"What can you mean, Sära?" he inquired. "I certainly thought Miss Meers had been invited to the ball, and was somewhat hurt because she did not come."

Mrs. Hartman shot a swift glance towards her lord and master. "Men do not understand women as women do each other," she replied dryly.

"Can you not be more explicit? What can the child have done to deserve ostracism?"

"Child? A pretty old child!" exclaimed his wife with raised brows.

"She is only seventeen," Mr. Hartman replied quietly.

"Seventeen! She is twenty if a day, and she has the worldly wisdom of fifty. She reminds me of an adventuress in a play."

Mr. Hartman paled with suppressed anger. His wife's words and tone were disappointing and exasperating. It was the first time he had caught a glimpse of the sly little moth that had eaten into the white feathers of his angel's wing.

"I insist upon less enigmatical statements," he said emphatically, rising from the table as he spoke. "I thought you were the girl's friend, Sära."

This was terrible! To have her son's heart ensnared was bad enough, but when her husband began to defend a woman against the attack of her tongue, matters had gone entirely too far. She must make a telling shot.

"I have promised to befriend her certainly, dear," was her sweet response. "You discovered her talent and naturally I wanted to please and aid you. But that does not put me under obligations to acknowledge socially a woman of whose past life I am entirely ignorant."

Mr. Hartman was somewhat appeased by the softly flattering tone and fondly proud smile of the woman he adored.

"I think you are a trifle too strict, Sära," he replied in a milder voice. "Miss Nana has little past to speak of, and I consider her one of the most simple and honest young ladies of the Academy."

"But you must own that she is not refined. How about the bad breeding she exhibited in passing up and down before our house in company with a pack of other loud creatures the night of our wedding? I consider it disgraceful, and should I introduce her to our friends, would she not time and again put me to shame?"

"Could you not help to form her manners? Is not her behavior in this matter to which you refer her only offense?"

"No! Not by any means! News was brought me several months ago how she one night in company with a person of questionable position, went out and peddled newspapers on the street."

Mr. Hartman looked sober for a moment, then resumed the defense of his favorite student.

"It may be all a mistake. It is all a mistake I feel certain. Besides, Sära, if the girl is inclined to be erratic, she is all the more in need of your personal supervision—all the more in need of love and kindness. She should not be living unchaperoned in a boarding-house. Why don't you bring her here, and treat her as a daughter?"

Worse and worse! What would the blind, misguided man suggest next?

"Really, my dear, for a man of your experience, your ignorance of human nature is astonishing. You are so good yourself that you can not believe ill of others. *I* train the girl? She would not allow herself to be trained. She has a most ungovernable tem-

per, depend upon it. All such undisciplined creatures
have.''

"Nevertheless I think we ought to try, Sära," said
Mr. Hartman, letting his hand fall caressingly upon
her crispy, golden hair.

Mrs. Hartman smiled up at him with tears in her
bright little eyes. Her last sip of tea had gone wrong
in her gulp of desperate indignation, but no matter,
the tears it brought would serve another purpose.

"I will promise, to please you dear," she replied
with a kiss.

The newspapers escapade had been reported to
Mrs. Hartman by an acquaintance shortly after its
occurrence, but that lady had smiled indulgently and
let it pass. It was only a girlish freak. Now however, it would be an excellent tool in her hand, for she
had set herself about to pick a quarrel with the girl
and anger her into bad behavior that she might have
an excuse for maintaining the position she had taken
with regard to her *protegèe*. She accordingly summoned Nana to her at once.

"What is this I hear?" she began in a high-keyed
voice freighted with displeasure. "You have been
betraying my confidence, and acting both ungratefully
and unbecomingly. Mr. Hartman is very much dis-
pleased as well as myself."

"What have I done?" inquired the girl. She
had in her surprise quite forgotten her behavior the
night of the ball.

"What have you not done? Miss Meers, I thought
that you were a lady."

"I hope I am, Mrs. Hartman, and I am sorry that I have done anything to displease either you or Mr. Hartman."

The other woman sneered slightly, and continued:

"Is it the mark of a lady to go past the houses of her benefactors with a mob of loud young women creating a disturbance, when a reception is going on?"

Nana flushed. "Indeed Mrs. Hartman," she said, "I have wished again and again that I had not done it, though the young ladies with whom I walked were not loud, only good-natured and so full of life that some of it must bubble over. They meant no harm. They did not know they were disturbing any one. There were only six of us."

"And six too many. I trust that I shall never be obliged to complain of such conduct again, or really Miss Meers, if I should, Mr. Hartman insists that something must be done. He said he was afraid that you were becoming wild and in need of strict supervision."

Her look and tone would have incensed a less spirited girl than Nana. She blushed to the roots of her hair feeling how unjust was the accusation, but she said nothing.

"I don't wonder you hang your head and keep silent," her tormentor went on.

This was more than Nana could endure without a protest.

"I think you are very unkind, Mrs. Hartman," she said. "Is this not the only thing I have been guilty of?"

"No," said the lady impressively. "News has lately been brought me that you—you, Miss Meers were seen a while ago in company with a low person, peddling newspapers on the street. Do not deny it. I have it on good authority."

"I do not deny it, only I will say that I did not peddle the papers and that I was not in any low company. It was a deed of kindness to a little sick newsboy, not my idea, but that of the lady who was with me."

"And who, pray was the—ahem—lady?"

"Thalia Sedling," Nana replied in a reverent half whisper.

"That bold creature! That actress!" Mrs. Hartman shrieked.

"Mrs. Hartman," said Nana, "I can not let anything be said to me against my dead friend, the woman that you, least of all, should speak ill of."

Mrs. Hartman winced. "I am astonished," she returned, with all the dignity she could summon up, "I am astonished Miss Meers, at the way in which you talk to persons who are older than you."

"I can't see how age has anything to do with it. We are all bound to respect the dead, and I will say one thing more. If you knew Miss Sedling as I knew her, you could not fail to acknowledge, if you were honest about it, that she was a better woman than either you or I."

With this parting fling, Miss Meers turned abruptly, and left the room.

CHAPTER XII.

THALIA'S OLD STUDIO.

MRS. HARTMAN was only fifteen years older than her handsome son, and looked almost as young and fresh as he. She had taken life easy, and it left her at thirty-nine plump and rosy, with the same careless, girlish toss of head that had captured the hearts of many a luckless swain in the days when the city of L. was new. She was her mother's daughter, and had married early as girls in new countries where women are scarce are apt to do, the man who among her suitors had the largest bank account. He was more than thrice her age, and she was early widowed. Sorrow sat lightly upon her. Tears shed in a lace handkerchief lose half their bitterness.

The widow had not been anxious to choose a second mate. Her weeds were becoming ; she had all of the world's goods that she needed ; she could afford now, she told herself, to wait and marry for love. She was surrounded by admirers of all classes whose adulation was even more sweet to her than that of those who did her homage when she was a debutante. With some persons, capacity for enjoyment increases with the years. Mrs. Star was one of these.

Such was Sära, the social goddess, when she met Mr. Hartman, king of the little art world of L. Like

others of her type, she was easily captivated by anything that was called genius, providing it was coupled
with a pleasing personality. Mr. Hartman, in turn,
was fascinated by her beauty and apparent power, her
youthful airs that were so refreshing, her artistic gowns
and luxurious atmosphere, and so as stories usually
end, they were married.

It was at the tea-table the evening of the day on
which Mrs. Hartman had talked with Nana.

"I told you so!" exclaimed the brilliant lady as
she met her husband's inquiring glance. "That girl
is uncontrollable. I sent for her this afternoon to advise with her in a friendly way, and see if my influence
could soften her in any degree, but she met me like
a thunder gust, spat fire at me like a little dragon.
She was impertinent, not to say insulting." Mrs.
Star's voice failed here. She sat back in her chair
and fanned herself vigorously.

"What did she say Sära?" Mr. Hartman inquired
gravely.

"What didn't she say? Oh that I should ever
have been born to listen to such words from one I've
tried to help! She accused me of dishonesty, of
dishonesty, Mr. Hartman, and declared that the
woman who sold papers on the street with her was a
better woman than I ever thought of being!" Mrs.
Hartman closed her eyes with a gasp and slight shud-
der.

"I am so sensitive," she continued with a sigh.
"Poor ma used to say that I'd never live to see forty,

things affected me so. I wonder the little hussy didn't strike me in the face. She looked as though she might any minute, but I bore up bravely and said my say as gently as I could under the circumstances. I have tried to help the girl, I have indeed, Mr. Hartman. I have done my best, I've done all she'd let me do!" She plied her fan again, and moaned slightly.

"Don't distress yourself so, my dear," answered her husband with sorrow and affection. "You must eat your supper and so must I. Let us dismiss all unpleasant topics for the time. Later on we'll see what can be done. I am sorry, I am truly sorry that I should have been mistaken in the girl, and should have urged your undertaking in the first place anything that could perchance turn out annoying to you. I must insist on her making you a proper apology—"

"Oh, Mr. Hartman, do not be rash! The girl will never apologize. She would die in the street first. They all would, those untrained creatures. I have undertaken to educate her and she has been pampered, pampered mind you, and it would be too cruel to throw her upon the world after that. I will still be her benefactoress, but I must insist upon placing money in the bank at her disposal, and allow my lawyer to transact all business between us. I really can't see her again—never!"

"How generous you are Sära," said Mr. Hartman, reaching across the table to stroke the white jeweled hand that was busy with the tea-cups. His wife gave him an affectionate smile, and peace reigned again in the Star-Hartman establishment.

Bernard Star, who had been sullenly munching a crust of dry bread, quite indifferent to its taste, so that it kept him occupied, looked on with silent disapproval; but he was afraid of his mother and ventured not a word.

Nana had gone home feeling tired and old. She had walked very fast, had almost run. When she caught sight of her white face and glassy eyes in the hall mirror, she paused a moment to assure herself that the reflection was really hers, after which she hurried to her room and threw herself upon a couch to think. Think! Her head was bursting with the surging thoughts that jostled one another in her brain. Life—what was its object? The only answer to that question her heart would give seemed to be, "We are born to suffer."

She had been ready to love Mrs. Star as a mother. She had craved her love and guidance. She needed it. She had never known a mother's love, and the hope that another woman's might take its place had been very sweet to her.

Then too, she was under obligations to Mrs. Hartman. Her weary eyes wandered about her rooms. They were furnished according to her taste, and were everything that an artistic soul could wish; but she would not, could not keep them now. How could she?

"I am only seventeen," she said, turning heavily on her bed, "only seventeen yet how old I am! I have lived a lifetime. Oh Louise, Louise, how fortunate you were to die!"

The sound of her dead friend's "own old name" seemed to give her courage.   She sat up, and pushing back the hair from her hot forehead, began to plan for a change of living.   She knew of a place where she could get orders for painting Christmas cards, and now and then a design for a fan to make.   She could have Miss Sedling's old, undesirable quarters for six dollars per month, and could cook her own food as Thalia had done.   Perhaps she should soon die as Thalia did.   She cared little what became of her ; life was too disappointing and difficult.

The shadows began to gather in the room.   Nana did not realize how late it was.   She let an hour and a half more go by without stirring, and was very much surprised when the bell in the town hall rang out seven, and the chambermaid knocked at the door to ask if she did not intend coming to supper.

Mrs. Hartman had not reckoned the strength of the mettle with which she had to deal.   On the following day, Nana sought a private interview with the husband of the great lady, her old instructor and friend.   He met her with a grave, severe face.   Nana had never looked into his eyes before except to meet a smile. She understood the situation.

" Mr. Hartman," she began somewhat timidly, " I have something to say to you."

" By what I have been hearing, I should judge that you ought to have," was the cold reply.

" I want to tell you something," she went on, her sense of justice rising to help her in that trying moment. "I want to speak to you because you have been a friend, and I care for your good opinion. What I have to say may do no good. It probably will not; but I want to know if you are aware who the woman was that your wife objected to my associating with, the one who, as she puts it, sold papers on the street?"

"I do not know," said Mr. Hartman. "I judged by what I heard that it was some chance acquaintance."

"It was Thalia Sedling."

Mr. Hartman looked up with a start.

"Impossible!"

"No, it is not impossible. You know and I know that no truer heart ever beat than hers."

"I know it," replied the artist softly.

"She carried papers to nineteen or twenty houses to help a little Irish boy who was ill with a fever."

Mr. Hartman looked uneasy. He fingered the cardboard and brushes on the table before him with nervous hands.

"Mrs. Hartman must have made some mistake," he stammered. "She was probably misinformed."

"She made no mistake," said Nana. "I told her who my companion was and also the purpose of the act. As Thalia herself said, it was not a ladylike thing to do. The refined and cultivated way to dispose of the case would have been to shed a few tears or give the little fellow a penny or two, and after that leave him to lose his customers and starve."

Nana's voice rang through the room like a pæan. Her friend was dead but the strength of her spirit lived in the girl whose life she had helped to shape. Tears gathered in her instructor's eyes. The deed and the words were so like Thalia Sedling that he could not doubt the truth of the story. He coughed to help cover his emotion.

"It must have been a mistake—Mrs. Hartman could not have understood," he repeated helplessly.

"She did understand. I told her plainly enough for anyone to understand. Do you not understand me perfectly?"

"Yes."

"Is Mrs. Hartman's understanding less acute than yours?"

"Ahem, ahem!" coughed Mr. Hartman. "Indeed Miss Nana, don't you think you are inclined to be a trifle hard on Mrs. Hartman? She has befriended you, she wishes you well. She was very much grieved at your manner and words yesterday and—and—"

"What was my manner and what were my words?"

Mr. Hartman hesitated and looked perplexed.

"What were my words?" Nana repeated, glaring at him like an irate and determined Nemesis.

"Well—ahem! Didn't you accuse her of being dishonest—and—"

"It is false. My words have been twisted around to make a better story."

"Ah—do you realize Miss Meers, that the lady of

whom you are speaking is my wife? Do you forget
that she has been your protectress? What possible
wish could Mrs. Hartman have to injure you?"

"That I can not tell; but she has one."

"As I said before, Mrs. Hartman was very much
grieved. But she is willing to let by-gones be by-
gones and forgive you if there is indeed anything to
forgive. I myself do not doubt that there has been
much misunderstanding all around. I think it would
be better to let it all pass. Mrs. Hartman will still be
your friend. She told me last night that she would.
She is very generous and—"

"And one thing more I will say," Nana interrupted,
"I came this morning chiefly to tell you that Mrs.
Hartman's generosity will not be taxed any more by
me. I have found employment and will hereafter
take care of myself. I have arranged to occupy
Thalia Sedling's old room, with the same privileges
that she had, and will move my few belongings there
to-day. The things purchased with Mrs. Hartman's
money, she may take charge of or leave alone as she
pleases. I shall make no more use of them."

"Are you—ahem! Are you not a trifle hasty?
Had you better not take time to reflect? Think of
the life you are choosing—one full of disappointment
and deprivation. Think of Miss Sedling's early
death—" here something choked him, and Nana was
given an opportunity to answer.

"I have thought of it all, but my mind will never
change."

Night found Nana duly installed in the little bare room once occupied by the one whose home was now the white, silent city of countless inhabitants. The moon looked down through the sky-light upon her uninviting couch in the corner. There was the faded little curtain behind which Thalia had kept her small oil stove and cooking utensils. The floor had a rag mat on it, and but for that was wholly uncovered. The clicking of her shoes upon the wood as she walked about, filled the girl with loneliness. The apartment was so empty and still that it seemed alive with echoes made by the sound of her every movement. She had half expected to feel the old dear influence of her friend's presence, which was one of her chief reasons for choosing the place; but it was not there, the comforting superstition was dispelled, and into her heart crept in its stead, a feeling of desolation for which the echoes showed no mercy.

The bread of freedom was not sweet to Nana, and the tea prepared by her own hands was insipid and vile. The first night of her emancipation was not a happy one. She felt no thrills of joy at thought of liberty. She saw life stretching out before her monotonous and blank. She had not Thalia Sedling's self-nurtured stoicism to help her bear it. Her coarse pillow-case formed the acquaintance of salt water that night if it had never before known the lachrymal fluid.

All night she listened to the rumble of car-wheels and whistle of engines, for the house in which she had taken up her abode was not many blocks from the

railroad.   She heard the town clock strike every
hour.   Just as the day began to break, she fell asleep,
and was awakened about eight o'clock by a rapping
at the door, and a voice calling:

"Miss Sedling—I would say Miss Meers—the
postman has been here and has left two letters."

Nana received the creamy perfumed envelopes, and
listlessly broke the seals.   The first one read:

Nana, my dear child, we were all mistaken.   My husband
has thoroughly investigated matters and has found out the
exact truth of the story.   You should not have been so hasty,
darling girl.   I know it was the result of your impulsive
nature, or I should never forgive your last step.   Come back
to us.   We cannot do without you.   Can you do without us ?
Can you renounce an easy path to your desired goal?   I was
just contemplating inviting you to my house as soon as your
period of severe study should be over, to introduce you to
society as my daughter, my very own little girl, when this
dreadful thing occurred.   Will you not consent to forget it
all, as we all wish to do ?
                    Your loving friend,
                              SARA HARTMAN.

The other letter was addressed in a long effeminate
hand.   It was from Bernard Star.

MY DEAR MISS MEERS :—

Jolly, what a lark !   I have been chuckling for an hour
over it.   It is good as anything I ever read in *Puck*, by Jove!
The mater is squelched if she ever was in her sweet life.   To-
day, the pater came home stern and cold as an icicle, and
told her in firm tones that she'd made a mistake about you
and would better write and take everything back.   The
mater shed tears but the pater remained unmoved.   The

mater's afraid if she brings you to the house I'll marry you, by Jove, and she is right. The pater is a trump! He has good strong principles and I admire him, with all my soul, even if he is my step pa, don't you know. By the beard of Mahomet the Just, the show that we had here was better than a base ball game. The mater will write and ask you to come to our house and you are to be a *debunté*, and what a dear little one you'll make, by Jove. But I shall not allow you to have many fellows dangling after you, even if I have to fight a duel with every man in L. Now, Nana, be good, and come back to us. You showed lots of pluck by leaving, and I admire your policy. I couldn't believe my eyes you had so much. It was just the proper thing to bring them to their senses. I would never have dared to go on loving you if the mater had not changed her key-note. You see how it would have been all round if things had not come about just so. I should have had to be miserable all my life.

There is going to be a Russian Tea at the Palladian to-night as I suppose you are aware. I will send you some flowers, and meet you at the table. Sorry I can't come before, but I've promised a fellow to go fishing this afternoon, and won't be back till late.

Yours forever in word and deed,

BERNARD STAR.

CHAPTER XIII.

THE CAMP MEETING, AND WHAT AN OLD BOOK TOLD.

A T the Royster farm things had gone on as usual with but few variations. Lund lay buried out among the hills he loved so well. Rose Dolby had been made happy by at last receiving her father's consent to her marriage with Bub, for Mr. Dolby was touched by his daughter's loyalty, and had given in. Lucky Fielding went about haggard and hopeless. Ever and again he made another fruitless excursion to the city; not the slightest clue of Nana could be found.

Time served only to strengthen his devotion. She was gone, he was at fault, he loved her. These were the thoughts that seldom left his mind. Was she dead, or worse than that was she alive and struggling under burdens too hard for one so young to bear? Perhaps by this time, she had forgotten him and loved some one else. The thought was bitter.

As he sat disconsolate one evening in the gathering twilight, he thought of Lund, and wondered how she would feel did she know the fate of her childhood's nearest companion, especially did she know how he had loved her. After a time, Lucky rose, and strolled listlessly over the hills to the lonely mound which marked the silent dwelling place of the boy whose life had been meek even to weakness. Long he stood, contemplating the narrow rise of earth; a tear gathered in his eye, and rolled down his cheek. At length, he turned slowly away, and started back home by the old freight road. He had not gone far when the sound of voices rang out loud and clear singing enthusiastically:

"Follow, follow, I will follow Jesus,
    Anywhere, everywhere I will follow on."

It was an itinerant religious organization known as the "Crusaders," who had pitched its tent on the hillside and was calling in from all quarters of the settlement both scoffer and repentant sinner, the one to make sport, the other to drink in with thirsty hearts the good news brought by these self-forgetting evangelists.

Lucky had not intended to visit their meetings, but finding himself thus close at hand, he drew near partly from curiosity, and partly because his heart was sad from loss of Nana and subdued by thoughts of Lund.

As he approached the tent, he saw the form of Rose Dolby, her face bowed upon her hands, and near her knelt Mrs. Royster, alternately groaning and wiping the tears from her lusterless eyes. Bub was here, leaning against a post, his countenance hard and immobile. A white-faced girl in blue gown and poke bonnet was pleading with him, but Bub was as rigid as Mahomet's mountain.

In the rear of the tent, another blue-gowned woman was kneeling by the side of a particularly sinful man who had come from Elk Bend "to see the show."

He was a frequenter of the one little gambling den at the Bend, and woe to any man who took a hand against him in "high five." Billy Wonder would pay for all the drinks, if only the stakes were high enough. This woman now arose and spoke. Her voice was of a pure reverberant quality, and as it thrilled through the tent, Lucky Fielding bent forward listening eagerly.

"My friends, here is a fellow-man who bids me speak for him. He has sinned deeply and has deeply repented. He is not ready as yet to declare his salvation, with his own tongue, but bids me tell you that he has cast all his burdens at the feet of the Lord, and has been given in return that complete rest of heart, that peace which passeth understanding. Oh my friends, you who are world-weary, you who are heavy laden come now, and like our happy brother here, take upon yourself the yoke of Him who was meek and lowly, and learn how easy it is to bear. Why will you remain troubled, why will you remain over-burdened when He has promised to bear it all for you, and give you all you ask of Him? 'Whatsoever you ask in My name believing, that will I do,' saith the Lord."

"Praise God!" was echoed through the crowd, and Lucky awoke from a moment of almost absolute oblivion to surroundings, to find himself kneeling among the rest with this prayer surging to his lips,

"Oh Lord, I've been a sinner, I've been a rank sinner, but from this day forth, I'll be a better man.

Forgive me if you can, and give me back my little girl."

The prayer was never breathed aloud, for at this instant, a terrific shriek rose from one corner of the tent; looking up, he saw Mrs. Royster erect and clinging to the tent ropes with one hand, while the other was raised beseechingly to heaven.

"O my God!" she cried in agony, "Spare me just a little while! Spare me, wicked sinner that I am, and I'll promise that I'll tell all—all!"

Every eye was upon her, and the tent was still as death. Bub was beside her in a twinkling. Loosing the fiercely clinging hands, he muttered something about the woman's being crazy, and bore her away like a child, through the crowd and out of the tent.

*   *   *   *   *   *

Whatever else the meeting may have done for Lucky, it had lifted up his heart and renewed his hope. The dusk of the next day found him again in the city following his quest. His search was not methodical now as it used to be. He asked no aid of the police. Instead of watching shop doors at the end of working hours, or those of churches before and after service, he loitered about the streets at random, scanning the faces of persons he met. He made few inquiries. They had never done any good. The unuttered prayer of yesterday kept welling up in his heart. Now and then he smiled bitterly at his own folly. "Fool, to think miracles are going to take place in an American city near the end of the nine-

teenth century ! Such things were for another age
and other men. Do you expect to bribe God to
change his plans, by promises of future goodness,
fool? What will your prayers amount to when
Lund's were of no avail? God helps those who help
themselves. Stop this nonsense, and have some aim
and reason in your work." These were his thoughts
as he roamed about. When he first entered the
streets of L. that day, he had in truth, expected to
meet Nana face to face. His period of religious
exaltation began to wane, and he laughed now, at
what he called his superstition.

Thus he had been walking the tiresome streets for
about three hours, when he fell into a little by-way, a
sort of connecting link between two more business-like
places. He was beginning to feel faint from hunger
and weariness, and to wonder concerning the shortest
cut to some comfortable lodging-house, when he came
upon a little rickety old building, so desolate and
tumble-down even beside the others, that he felt
almost sorry for it; with its rugged storm-battered
face, it looked to him almost human in its wretched-
ness. It was only his mood, of course, that made it
appear so. The dim light of a gas-lamp in front of it
fell upon the sign:

OLD BOOKS,

CHOICE TEN CENTS.

Lucky had no thought of purchasing, but moved by
his innate love of books, he began to turn over the
dusty volumes. There was one of an unusually inter-

esting title. He picked it up to examine its pages, when all at once he noticed in dim penciling on one of the margins a handwriting which he thought he knew. Holding it to the light, he studied it closely, and by perseverance was enabled to decipher the characters. It was the name and address of Nana Meers.

"What do you want?" gruffly inquired the owner of the store, perceiving the length of Lucky's stay, and beginning to grow suspicious.

"Nothing," Lucky replied in a tone that sent the unsophisticated bookseller into a spasm of blind wonderment, "Nothing in the world."

Lucky did not take time to consider whether this was only a remarkable coincidence, or an indirect answer to his prayer. He was no longer tired, no longer hungry. Like a newly freed prisoner, he sped over the ground only stopping now and then to inquire the way of some astonished denizen of the side streets in which he so often found himself. Another half-hour, and he was at the door of the house where Nana had lodged after her departure from the Bonds', previous to her acquaintance with Mrs. Star.

"I can't tell you where she lives now," the woman who answered his ring replied to his eager questioning. "Are you a friend of hers?"

"Yes," Lucky answered, his heart sinking again. "I am an old friend from the country. I haven't seen her for a year and am very anxious. Didn't she tell you where she was going?"

"She did but I forget. Margaret, Margaret!"
she called turning back into the hall.

A young woman very shortly appeared wrapped in
a shawl. She had a wheezy voice, and carried a
saucer with some smoking cubeb berries in it. She
eyed the stranger curiously.

"Where did that Miss Meers go to after she left
here?" woman number one asked.

Woman number two stared at Lucky again, and
answered with much hesitation:

"Let me see. I have forgotten the street and
number, but I know that she's gotten rich since.
She's been adopted by some wealthy lady, I believe.
She's been studying to be an artist down at the Palladian Academy, corner of K and Fifth Street. You
are a friend of hers from somewhere, I suppose."

"Yes, an old friend."

"You wouldn't know her now I guess. I've heard
she's become quite a lady," the woman continued,
plainly evincing her eager delight in watching the
changes of expression that swept one after another
over Lucky's countenance. In an instant, she had
read the story, and was smacking her intellectual lips
over it, with the keen relish of a mental *savant.* What
after all is gossip? Just a supply originated to fill the
demand of the soul for morsels of life. Let no one
deny his appetite for it. It is moral salt. That it
may be taken in too large quantities for the health is
true, as it is with other condiments.

"You might go down to the Academy, and inquire.

They sometimes have night classes I believe, and somebody there, perhaps, could tell you where she lives now." She almost wished she could ask him to come back and let her know the result, but she dared not.

Lucky turned away not half so light of heart and foot as he had come, to seek the art building on the corner of K and Fifth Street, as directed. Nana had become rich! She was now quite a lady! How would she receive him, the friend of her less prosperous days? She probably had lovers by the score. He would see her at any rate, assure himself of her happiness, then if all were well he would go back to Elk Bend and try to rejoice in her good fortune. It was better than to find her dead or suffering, at any rate.

When he reached the Academy he found it ablaze with light, for the Russian Tea was in progress. Sounds of music and dancing issued from the windows. As Lucky paused before the street door, which stood ajar, he saw a lady and gentleman descend the hall stair. There was something familiar, yet unfamiliar about her. Was it Nana? It was taller than Nana, but—yes it was she.

They stood underneath the great chandelier in the hall. She spoke and smiled up at her escort, who took her hand and began to fasten her glove. He plucked a rose from her corsage, and they both laughed at something he said about it, after which they descended to the street and passed on. Lucky had only intended to look at her and go away, but he could not bring himself to do it. He could not let her go yet. He must keep her in sight a little while longer, then he would leave her and return home alone. He dropped in behind the couple, and followed them.

They had reached a small building surrounded by a picket fence, in the outskirts of the city. A pale light gleamed from one of the upper windows. "That is my studio," Lucky heard Nana say.

"Deuced bad looking place. You mustn't stay there long," said her escort. "Do you intend to?"

"I don't know," Nana answered somewhat sadly.

Her hand was upon the gate, but she was prevented from opening it by her companion, who put his arm about her, and drew her to him. This was too much for Lucky. Forgetting all his good resolutions, he stepped out of the darkness, and stood before them.

"And this is what I've spent days and nights the past year searching for!—Nana!"

They looked at him, the one in surprise, the other in blank amazement, but not for long. There was an expression of mingled love and pain in Lucky's face that was unmistakable. Nana did not wait to weigh pros and cons, or to think of the wife he was to have brought from the Upper Missouri. All that she remembered was that he was there and that she loved him. Releasing herself from Bernard Star's embrace, she ran to Lucky with outstretched hands.

"Oh, Lucky!" she cried sobbingly, "I love you, I love only you! Life is dreary, everything is dreary —take me home!"

CHAPTER XIV.

ALL THINGS COME ROUND TO HIM WHO WILL BUT WAIT.

MRS. ROYSTER had astonished the settlement. She had told a story which had set tongues to wagging with unwonted velocity. She had had dreams and visions, she said. Her dead husband had appeared to her, and commanded her to reveal all; so it gradually came out that all the Roysters possessed in the world was not theirs by right, but the property of Nana Meers.

Mr. Meers had been a scholarly man of very reticent manners not conducive to close friendships. He had kept a very good establishment in Philadelphia, and Royster had been his hostler and choreman. When Nana's mother had died, she, Jane Royster, had served as nurse, as she also did when Mr. Meers lay upon his death bed. His decease was sudden and unexpected, but they had no hand in that, the woman vowed with groans and sobs. His ailment was pneumonia, and the doctor who attended him could swear that he died a natural death. What Royster did do was this; he forged papers conveying the dying man's property and even the custody of his only child to "my trusted servants, Robert Royster and wife." Mr. Meers had no relatives, so the scheme prospered.

The arrangement seemed as suitable as any, to lookers-on. The child might have fallen into worse hands was the comment of acquaintances.

To avoid any questioning that might chance to occur in the future, they had as soon as possible, moved west, taking the child with them. They had kept her in ignorance of her birth, but she had always been an unwelcome reminder of their guilt. They hated her for this reason, and treated her accordingly.

By and by, they had purchased the dairy farm and prairie adjoining, and as time went on, they began to forget that their means of subsistence was ill-gotten. Nana came to be looked upon as an interloper, and they had been only too ready to accept Joe Slocum's overtures when he signified his desire to marry the girl, especially since he was willing to pay for her keep while growing up. This was Mrs. Royster's confession.

Bub averred that his mother's mind was failing, and had her locked up in an upper room of the house. There were no proofs against him, only a crazy woman's word, yet all the neighbors believed him guilty, and Bub soon found himself on the verge of ostracism.

Out under the eaves of her father's house in the cool of the evening, Rose Dolby sat and sewed. Her work was a very interesting garment of fleecy white; but her face was sad for the face of one whose fingers were busy with the seams of her own wedding gown.

Through the lively discussion going on everywhere

concerning her lover, Rose had been singularly quiet and had proceeded as before with the preparations for her marriage. She was as much talked of as Bub, and now and then, on her occasional visits to town, she was stared at and pointed out as "that Dolby girl, the one who is going to marry that Royster."

If all this hurt her, she showed no sign, and even her mother dared not question her on the subject.

The sun went down, and across the marshes, came Bub to call upon his betrothed. She had sent for him that afternoon. She responded composedly to his rather sheepish "Good-even," and requested him to sit down by her side. There was a long silence during which he fidgeted, and fumbled his hat brim while Rose remained calm and self-possessed. At length Bub spoke:

"Now Rose, what on earth do you want of me?"

"I've talked to you before, Bub," she answered quietly, "and I want to know what you have done, or what you intend to do. Have you made it all right with Nana Meers?"

"Hain't done nothin' to Nane, have I?"

"Bub," went on the girl in a firm voice, "I have loved you a long time and have trusted you even when other folks told me I was wrong. I never believed any of the stories about you, but this one I must believe. I can't cheat myself into thinking you're innocent. I can't believe you've done right by your poor mother to call her crazy and lock her up. Oh

Bub, won't you for my sake do the right thing? Give
Nana what belongs to her, and let's be happy!"

"Curse the girl!" growled Bub. "I wish she'd
never been born. She's kicked up a hulabaloo all her
life, and is likely to go on in the same way till she
dies."

Rose looked at him with cold critical eyes.

"Do you intend to make it all right?" she asked
almost sternly.

"And make a beggar of myself?"

"Yes, if it is the right thing to do, and I believe in
my heart it is."

"Now look here, Rose," argued Bub, "what if the
money in the first place did belong to Nana's father?
Who is it that's improved the farm and made it worth
something, and who has housed and fed her? Why,
we've earned the farm and things six times over by
the trouble she's caused the past year, the vixen!"

"And whose fault was it that she made the trouble?
Who gave you the right to sell her to Joe Slocum?
For it was just the same as selling as I see it."

Bub cringed for an instant, then stood up and
glowered at Rose with all his might. She was
becoming domineering and needed to be taught her
place. A woman often did.

"I won't do it," he said in blustering tones, "not
for you nor any other woman. You think you've got
me under your thumb, but we'll see."

He was scarcely prepared for Rose's firm reply.

"Then we must part, Bub."

"Well, part it is then," he retorted, and turning his back upon the Dolby house, shuffled off, expecting fully, however, to be called back before he should get out of hearing; he had so long been accustomed to Rose's forgiving tenderness.

This time he was mistaken. Rose watched him out of sight with set, determined lips. Presently her mother joined her, and questioned softly:

"How much more to sew, dear?"

Rose answered wearily:

"I think, mother, I won't sew any more. I'll put this dress away. Somehow, since the day pa brought it home, I've thought I'd never wear it. You remember the time, mother. That was his loving way of consenting to our marriage, mine and Bub's. But I wasn't happy as I expected to be. There's lots of tears wrapped up in that sewing that no one knows of. Mother, Bub has been here and I've sent him home. We'll never be married at all unless—unless he should make up his mind to do the right thing."

Rose had risen to her feet. Her mother took her cold hands.

"You have done right, Rose," she whispered, "My brave child, you have done right."

Rose's countenance changed in an instant. It became hard and deadly white, and before her mother could utter another word, she had fallen limply to the ground burying her face in her wedding dress.

"Don't speak to me!" she shrieked sobbingly. "Don't say a word! I loved him. God only knows

how I loved him.   It's no small thing to me, and
praise ain't any comfort.   Don't say a word to me!''

  * * * * * *

Lucky Fielding had seen Bub Royster cross the
swamp to farmer Dolby's house, and an idea had
entered his mind which he soon hastened to put into
execution; going into the machine-shed, he brought
out the hide of an ox newly cured, to which head and
horns were still attached.

"Where are you going?" asked Nana, now his
wife, as she espied him walking off with the queer
bundle under his arm, chuckling to himself meanwhile.

"Oh, just to have a little fun with Bub Royster,"
was the careless reply, and Lucky strode away in the
direction of the swamps before Nana could protest.

It had grown quite dark when Bub began to make
his way across the swamps.   He was stalking along
morosely, his head fallen upon his chest, when he
heard the sound of deep breathing at his side, and
looking up, he saw a sight that caused a chill to seize
the roots of his hair.

A great hairy monster with long tail and wide-
spreading horns stood there close enough to touch.
Bub's superstitious fear augmented the horror of it.
He would have fled, but the thing spoke, and Bub, in
his great fright, felt his feet rooted to the spot.

"Stop! Bub Royster," said the thing in sepulchral
tones, such as Bub had never before heard.   "Stop;
there's a little business matter that you and I must
settle before either of us is a day older.   I regret to

say that I haven't a card about me, but my name if you care to know, is Satan. We haven't had any previous acquaintance, but you've heard of me, and I've heard of you, so there's little use to stand on ceremony. You know, Bub Royster that you are a bad lot. Well, I'm the man that settles all points that legal processes can't reach, and I'm here to have it out with you. Are you ready for me?"

Bub's teeth chattered so that he could not speak.

"Come now, no dallying!" it went on. "I'm a man of business, and can't waste my time on snivelling little atoms of humanity like you. Are you going to settle up this little muddle you've gotten into, in the right manner, or shall I take you to roast for my Sunday dinner?"

Bub Royster trembled so that he could scarcely move, but finally managed to sink upon his knees before the thing, and, raising his hands in supplication, to exclaim:

"Oh Satan, oh, good Mr. Satan, let me go! I'll be a better man from this time on. I swear I will. I'll give Nane Meers the dairy farm and all the stuff, and I'll let my mother out. It wa'n't no lie, she told; it was gospel truth, and I'll fix it up all right if you'll only try me again."

"Thank you," replied the apparition with dignity. "Do as you say, and I'll not trouble you, but remember that I shall keep an eye on you, and if things are not quite satisfactory to my mind, you'll hear from me again."

With this it withdrew into a clump of alders near
at hand, and Bub was left to pick his way over the
marshes still trembling and starting every time the
rushes stirred, or a wary frog leaped into its home
pool at his approach.   A quarter of an hour later,
found Lucky Fielding relating to Nana, in the midst of
smothered chuckles, his success in the rôle of Beelzebub's master.

*   *   *   *   *   *

It was a bright, clear day in the early spring.   The
hills, from which the dead grass of the year previous
had been newly burned, were rich with mottled purple
and faint green.

"Who says we have no beauty of landscape here?"
said Nana.   "Who speaks of our prairies as bleak
and uninteresting?   Look ! every square yard of earth
is of a different hue.   Lucky, how many shades of
purple do you see on that hill?"

"It looks all the same to me," Lucky vowed at
first.   "But no," he added after further scrutiny;
"you are right, you are right, little one.   There's no
less than a dozen, though I never thought enough
about it to notice them before.   Upon my word, what
a girl you are, Nana."

"So it is in life," went on the little philosopher.
"We must look many times before we can see the
real beauty of some people."

They were ascending by the broad track of the
great freight road, the hill on the opposite side of
which, Lund lay in his long slumber.   Lucky was

happy, even gay.   He had scored some very brilliant successes politically of late, and the district had begun to talk of him as the future member of the House in the State Legislature.   He was a general favorite, and the career which his ambition craved seemed already within his grasp.   By his side she too, would shine, his beautiful, talented wife, augmenting his glory. His thoughts were more of himself than of the quiet sleeper beyond.

"Well, Bub and Rose are married by this time," he remarked carelessly as they walked along; "it's almost four o'clock, and you said the ceremony was to be at half past three.   He can't be the hero he used to be in her eyes.   I wonder that she marries him.   She could have done better.   That's what the Hartmans might have said of you, eh Nana?   But then as to poor Rose, she loved the fellow, as you do me, perhaps, and since she can't have him with the halo that she used to see around his head, she'll take what she can get, and try to imagine the rest."

"It is often so," Nana responded.   "But do you remember what Mrs. Browning says about such things?   'God keeps a niche in heaven to hold our idols, albeit he break them to our faces, and deny that our close kisses shall impair their white.' "

"We don't have to wait so long as that for our success and happiness, do we?   Only to think of the good fortune coming to us !   I'm certain to be elected, and you'll come out in the finest gowns any one ever saw. Mrs. Hartman and that Bernard Star will open their eyes,

I'm thinking, when they see you the wife of a states-man, instead of the stupid farmer they fancy you've married. The State Legislature is only a step, too—there's Congress, you know. I'll only have to say the word to get the nomination, when the time comes. Little girl, with your brains and good looks, you'll queen it over all Washington before you die."

"I am certainly pleased with your success," Nana answered. "God has been very good to us. I some-times wonder why, for there are those who have been more generous and noble, and have gained no praise. Their lives were not full of brilliant colors that chal-lenge the eye, but partook of those rich low tones which the careless observer never discerns. They must be studied to be appreciated, and few there are who will take the pains to do it."

Their conversation had been broken by intervals of silence, and by this time, they had reached the lonely mound, about which the buffalo grass was just begin-ning to peep, blade by blade. They paused at the head, where stood a small marble slab on which Lucky read for the first time the inscription which Nana had ordered to be chiseled there:

LUND
Aged 20.
He Was a Hero.

Lucky looked at Nana.

"You mean him," he said at length.

She nodded. Lucky moved a step nearer the grave and took off his hat.

Just then, across the hill, came a sound of merry voices, and the rumble of wagon wheels.

From grave to gay, from tears to laughter, from the bed of death to life at its full, this is the rule of mortal existence. We can not sorrow forever. Lucky and Nana turned to greet with congratulations the happy couple who came down the old freight road.

It was Bub and Rose returning from the minister's.

THE END.